PRAISE F

gain author A.M. Adair brings her two decades of e in the U.S. Intelligence community to bear on ther explosive novel. In this, the third installment of e Elle Anderson thrillers, ex-CIA agent Anderson is on run, pursued by a lethal terrorist and his allies as well as own government. Staying alive will be difficult, but more important than ever if she is to complete this, her most challenging mission ever. Adair keeps you breathless in anticipation in this exciting thrill ride, with new surprises galore. Action, drama, and political intrigue that can only be written by someone who has been there, done that. Adair has taken her craft to a new level as she gets better and better at keeping us on the edge of our seats!"

— Andrews and Wilson, international bestselling authors of the *Tier one, Sons of Valor,* and The Shepherds thriller series, as well as, *Rogue Asset,* their first installment in the WEB Griffin Presidential Agent Series.

"A.M. Adair has done it again! Another nail biter, with twists and turns that will knock you off balance. Although fictional, there are certain elements woven within the pages that only field experience can lend to the realism of the characters. *Shadow War* is fast paced and raw, both detailed and descriptive, leaving the reader captivated by and a longing for what the next page has ins pages turned, I felt as though I was pulle retirement! No shortage of emotion, *Shadow W* reader a bareknuckle operational experience th delivers as you'll find yourself shoulder-to-shoulde Elle Anderson. *Shadow War* garners my stro recommendation!"

—Robert E. Jordan, Chief Warrant Officer (R United States Navy, and author of *Faith, Flag, an Family: A Purposeful Guide for Selfless Service.*

"A.M. Adair is back with another hot action ride, kicking off the narrative with a tense and adrenaline-pumping action sequence and setting a violent and gripping tone for the latest Elle Anderson thriller, *Shadow War.*
Set only a few minutes after the events of *The Deeper Shadow*, Elle Anderson is targeted by a hit squad on orders of a renegade former CIA officer with a vendetta against her. Cut off from official resources, she has only her team to rely on as she takes the fight to her enemy. Outgunned and outnumbered, Elle and her team have to utilize every bit of their training and skillset to come out on top in this suicide mission.

Elle Anderson is a certified badass and there's no denying her profound impact in the thriller genre. A.M. Adair writes with the experienced hand of someone who has persevered through a plethora of tough situations as her protagonist does, both physically and emotionally. Elle Anderson's journey as a weathered spy is not without the realistic depiction of the toll of violence on the human psyche, regardless of how necessary it may be. Never during any part of the story did I feel Elle to be superhuman. That's not to say the action sequences were anything less than fantastic. A.M. Adair elevates both the quality and quantity of cinematic and tactically impressive shootouts with cutting-edge weaponry.

Shadow War is highly entertaining and utterly captivating with its smart plot and awesome characters, balancing fun with grounded emotional depth to create a memorable read. You'll be hard pressed to keep your jaw from dropping."

—***Kashif Hussain, Best Thriller Books***

"*Shadow War* is Adair's best work yet. What happens when you strip everything from someone like Elle Anderson, a highly-trained operative with world-class expertise in marksmanship, hand-to-hand combat, and tradecraft, and leave her with nothing to lose? You get a damn good story.

Shadow War picks up with Anderson taking up her most personal mission yet. And this time the battlefield in the greater D.C. Metro Area. Nonstop action, in-extremis planning, and on-the-fly operational changes will have you turning the pages to see what comes next. You'll trust no one and question everything as you follow Elle in this latest installment of the series.

Elle Anderson has the chops to keep up with the best. If you're a fan of James Reece, Mitch Rapp, Scot Harvath, and Max Ahlgren, then you're going to love Elle Anderson. Adair knows what she's writing about, and *Shadow War* proves that time and time again."

—Zach James, U.S. Army Veteran and author of Deception and its highly anticipated sequel Wetwork.

"You've got to meet Elle Anderson. She's my new crush. Seriously. And *Shadow War* is a white-knuckle, hold-on-for-dear-life, exhilarating ride from start to finish. Once you crack open the first page, you won't be able to put it down. It's definitely one of the most fast-moving books I've read in years. Maybe ever."

—Stan R. Mitchell, prior infantry Marine and author of ten military and police thrillers, including Sold Out: Nick Woods Book 1

AN ELLE ANDERSON NOVEL

SHADOW WAR

DAVE,
MISS ME YET? ☺
Ama Adair

A.M. ADAIR

STORY MERCHANT BOOKS
LOS ANGELES
2022

ISBN: 978-1-970157-32-1

Story Merchant Books
400 S. Burnside Avenue #11B
Los Angeles, CA 90036

www.storymerchantbooks.com

Interior format & cover design by IndieDesignz.com

AN ELLE ANDERSON NOVEL

SHADOW WAR

For all those who I have had the honor to serve with.

SHADOW WAR

PROLOGUE

CIA Headquarters, McLean, Virginia.

Four Years Earlier

Feigning contrition, Thomas Matthews looked around the Operations Directorate at the Central Intelligence Agency, taking in the faces of all his so-called colleagues. He wanted to remember every treacherous one. Their time would come. As he waited outside Director Marcus Calloway's office, his anger flared again, and he fought to keep his expression in check. Until just a few short months ago, he had been king here. They'd worshipped him. As they should. He was the rising star on the fast track to take over. Then she had shown up.

How had the fucking bitch survived?

It hadn't been the first time he had to remove a problem from his path. But it was the first time he'd failed, and it ate at him. The operation had been planned to perfection. He sent her after a cartel boss, her every move meticulously dictated and rehearsed. She was supposed to go into a communications blackout, infiltrate the group, and execute the target. After she went dark, Thomas had used the knowledge of her tasking and movements to leak information to the cartel that she was an undercover cop. He handed her to them on a silver fucking platter.

There was no way Elle Anderson should have been able to walk away from that assignment, let alone report him. But she had. Somehow, she made the group turn on each other, and slipped away. Worse, she brought back evidence that someone had tried to expose her. Someone with intimate knowledge of her operation. That was a short list. Suddenly, everyone was looking at him differently. They stopped telling him their secrets. His systems access was restricted while they investigated the accusations. He denied everything, but Calloway had always been threatened by him, and now the director had a new favorite. The evidence was circumstantial, but it would be enough to get him blacklisted if he stayed.

He always had a backup plan, but he hated that his hand was forced. The CIA was just a means to an end. He was destined for much bigger things. This was supposed to be a mere stepping stone to greatness. The resignation in his hand was a formality, but he needed to play this out.

The intercom on Kim Daniel's desk came to life. "Send him in."

"The director will see you now, Thom—Mr. Matthews," she said.

His blood pressure spiked. The insolence of Calloway summoning him so casually. After everything he'd done for this directorate. *Stay on task.* Rising to his feet, Thomas barely glanced at Calloway's secretary, the woman who'd been trying to get him into bed until a couple of days ago. She was ten years older than him and not nearly attractive enough, for starters...but sex hadn't been what he wanted from her—her value was in her connections.

Thomas walked into Calloway's office to see the man standing in the middle of the room—an armed security guard posted just inside the door.

"I'm not going to waste your time or mine, Mr. Matthews. The investigation is ongoing, and it is standard procedure to suspend account access and put all personnel involved in an administrative status until there is an official resolution. This process is not punitive. It's necessary. If your intent is still to submit your resignation, then I will accept it."

"I don't see Anderson going through the same thing that I am. You've already taken her side."

"Ms. Anderson is being fully debriefed and will then be placed on administrative leave. If your counter-accusation about her fabricating the report she filed is founded, then she will be brought up on charges, and you will be fully reinstated."

"If? How can you even entertain this?"

"All allegations of misconduct are taken seriously, Mr. Matthews. There is no room for compromise or uncertainty about the intentions of my agents when lives are on the line."

"And what about what you're putting me through with this lunacy? Am I just expected to shake everything off and move on as though I wasn't just betrayed and ostracized by everyone here?"

Calloway did not respond immediately. "Given the nature of the allegations and what we do here, you of all people should understand that a full investigation is the only way to move past this. An individual's pride is not a priority—particularly when it comes to the mission. You don't have to like it, but you do have to accept it. Now, what is your choice?"

Thomas paused long enough to give the impression that he was thinking it over but then held out the document and his security badge to Calloway. "I can't work like this."

"I'm sorry that it's come to this, Mr. Matthews, but I accept your resignation. If you have any personal items at your desk, you will be allowed to collect them, and then security will escort you out of the building."

The guard shifted his stance, indicating it was time to go. Thomas walked out of the corner office that should have been his someday, and he went to grab his bag. He felt eyes as he was escorted out of the building. After clearing the security checkpoint, Thomas watched as the guard slipped a thumb drive into his bag before handing it to him. Smiling, Thomas took the bag and walked away, satisfied. His first asset was in place and had performed flawlessly.

True power meant influence. Influence required information and the knowledge on how to apply it—this was what he was born to do. He'd been collecting valuable information his whole life, and now he had a treasure trove compliments of the CIA's databases. The information on the innocuous thumb drive was worth more than money, and he was going to use it to burn all his enemies to the ground. They would pay for interrupting his rise to power. He would come for all of them.

Especially Elle Anderson.

This isn't the end. It's the beginning.

CHAPTER 1

Monday, 2200: Outside Strasburg, Virginia.

Present Day

Nothing tests character like running for your life. Less than an hour ago, Elle Anderson had been lost in the depths of depression. After being dismissed from the CIA, she was adrift. Without purpose, she didn't know how to continue. Then the lights went out, literally.

The assault team had been lying in wait inside her house when they cut the power, hoping to capitalize on her weakened, emotional state. Her enemy had known where to apply pressure. Bringing her face-to-face with the source of all her nightmares: the chair. The one she had been bound, tortured, and almost killed in six months back. Her reaction to seeing it in her living room had been all-consuming, triggering the effects of post-traumatic stress she'd worked so hard to overcome. She walked right into their hands, and they used mind games to throw her off balance.

It almost worked.

Elle ran through the trees, escaping on foot, having killed an entire team of hitmen. She was thankful for the night vision goggles she'd taken from one of her would-be assassins. It would've been next to impossible to maintain her pace without them. But, as the view from the left eyepiece blurred again, Elle found herself wishing she could stop to wipe the blood-spatter (from the previous owner) off the lens. She hated having her vision obscured, particularly when she was being hunted. It was damned annoying. But she didn't have time to deal with it.

She'd killed six men tonight, and more were coming. The gunmen that had been inside the house had caught her unprepared. She'd been lucky to survive the assault. When the remaining members of the team chased her into the woods behind her house, she was ready for a fight by then—and four more bodies were added to the tally. Now, with all her senses on heightened alert, she was prepared for the next attack.

Elle was soaked from crossing the river, and some of the wetness had to be blood. Not all of it was hers, but she couldn't stop to assess the damage. She stumbled repeatedly but kept moving. Her body ached, and running was not helping the headache she had from the explosion she'd survived. Her car had been rigged to blow. Thank god for remote car starters and battle-honed intuition. The blast bought her precious seconds to escape what was left of her house without being mowed down by a barrage of bullets.

Thomas Matthews, ex-CIA operative turned terrorist mastermind, had arranged for his dogs to come after her.

His hatred was as irrational as it was potent. In his mind, Elle ruined him. She'd been the new rising star, and he couldn't allow anyone to challenge his position. That was the first time he'd tried to kill her. He failed but, apparently, would keep trying until one of them was dead.

Destroying her career and exposing her on the international stage wasn't enough. Elle would never be able to work in covert operations again because of him. But he still wanted her dead. His hitmen "welcoming committee" with their sniper, explosives, and automatic weapons had been ready for her. Tom was going to be incensed she survived their attack. But he had to have planned for her to make it through the first wave. More would be coming. *Where are they?*

The sound of a twig snapping was somehow louder than the ringing in her ears. Elle jumped behind the next tree in her path and froze, straining to listen. The forest had gone deadly silent. Even the faint hum of the insects had stopped. She was being hunted, and they were close. She considered her options: climb, run, or fight. They might miss her if she climbed but, if they didn't, she'd be trapped. Running meant drawing every gun her way instantly. She'd have to weave through the trees and pray a stray round didn't catch her. Then they would run her down or call in reinforcements to head her off.

The pistol in her hand had fourteen rounds plus one in the chamber. Another magazine was in her pocket. One gun versus heavily armed mercenaries wearing body armor, at night, in a forest; the odds were not in her favor.

This is it. Now or never.

Moving into a crouching position, Elle kept her motions slow and controlled to avoid making any noise. Her pursuers had to be equipped with thermal imaging to track her. Chances were better than average the only thing that had prevented them from shooting her had been the tree cover and her lead. They hadn't been able to line up a shot yet. Otherwise, she would've been dead already.

They'd be coming in single file through the trees and thick underbrush, following the man with the thermal camera, with alternating fields of fire. Elle would have one shot at most before all hell broke loose. The muzzle flash would give away her position to the rest of the team, but if she didn't take out the thermal camera, she'd never escape.

Glancing around, she mapped out her evasion route. Searching by the base of the tree, she found what felt like acorns. Grabbing a handful, she took a breath and launched into action. Throwing the acorns in one direction, she leaned out around the tree base the opposite way, weapon at the ready.

They were right on top of her.

Her stomach lurched at how close they were, but she didn't hesitate. Pivoting her aim upward, she struck the lead man in the face with two shots. There was a second man directly behind him. He whipped his weapon toward her and fired. Elle felt tree bark score her cheek as she pulled back behind it a fraction of a second before the rounds hit. Jumping to her feet, she moved around the tree and shot the second man in the side of his head before he could turn. The next man was about six feet away, and Elle heard him call out her position. She shot a series of four rounds for cover fire. Some bullets likely struck body armor, but she was on the move as soon as she pulled the trigger.

Making her way to the first man's body, Elle caught sight of the illuminated screen of the thermal camera and lunged for it. Diving across the path, she grabbed it and kept running on her pre-planned route. Seconds later, the forest exploded. Bullets shredded the foliage around her, sending debris hurling like shrapnel. Dropping to the ground, she army-crawled in a line perpendicular to her attackers, pulling herself along on her forearms and knees while maintaining control of the thermal camera and her pistol.

One of the men called for a ceasefire. Elle froze at the command. The voice sounded close. Turning the camera's screen toward the ground to avoid the light giving her away, she lay prone, listening.

"Spread out, find her," a gruff voice commanded.

Elle heard at least four people at close range. They were fanning out from their file into a line and would overtake her in moments. Pulling out a full magazine, Elle did a combat reload. Swapping the magazines in one fluid motion, she returned the half-empty one to her pocket. She couldn't risk wasting ammunition. Rolling over, she focused on the sounds of the movement closest to her. Someone was breaking through the underbrush, heading on a collision course with her in a few strides.

Raising her pistol, she estimated where her target would appear. Whoever gained their target first would win. The second the man's head came into view, she fired. The bullets ripped up through his chin, his body went slack, and he collapsed. The body scraped her leg when it fell, but Elle didn't move. Several rounds had been fired in response to her shot before their lead regained control.

"Who fired?" the leader asked.

"I didn't start it," a second man protested.

"Brian, Joe, sound off."

"I'm here," another man said, then silence.

"Joe?" Silence.

Three left to go. And they're trigger happy.

Elle did her best to estimate where her remaining targets were located. They would be converging on her position, and she needed to be ready. The lead was closest, somewhere to her right. The one who answered to Brian and the other guy were to her left. They had to know she was laid up, waiting for them, and would be hyper-vigilant. *Time to do something crazy.*

Staying low, Elle moved to the correct angle of approach. Then she launched herself in the direction of the lead man's voice, firing several rounds—just enough to give away her position. A round struck him in the chest. His body armor stopped the bullet, but the impact, still jarring, threw off his aim. As soon as she finished the third trigger pull, she dropped to the ground. The volley of shots passing over her head from the other two men accomplished what she wanted. The breaking brush, followed by a dull thud, told her the team lead had been taken out by friendly fire.

The ringing in her ears from the gunfire made the silence of the forest all the more pronounced. No one spoke. No one moved. The remaining two men were likely waiting for their leader to take charge, but the longer the silence stretched out, the more apparent it became that the man was gone. It was their move now. They had a general idea of where she was, but would they press on or retreat? Two against one, would they consider that enough of an advantage?

A slight rustling noise told her one of them was making a move.

"You'll never make it out of here, bitch."

How original. Idiot.

Give up now, and we'll make it quick," the idiot added.

It was the whiny shooter. He couldn't have been more than fifteen feet away, but it might as well have been a mile. She wouldn't be able to use the same tactics again. They were stupid but not that stupid. New plan.

She started laughing. "Oh, sweetheart. That's cute. You have no idea what you were hired for, do you?"

No response.

"You're not here to take me out. You're here to see how fast I can kill you. This is an audition of sorts, and you're just the pawns. Or did you really think it was normal to send twelve men after one woman? Team one didn't last long enough to even give me a workout."

There was a long pause before the man said, "You're lying."

"You didn't know about the first team, did you? Figures. They didn't want you to back out. Well, your four dead companions should be enough to clue you in. You guys were conned. Even if you had managed to take me out, you'd be dead men, anyway. No loose ends allowed.

It's almost enough to make me want to let you walk away."

Waiting on their next move, the hum of the forest started to pick back up around her. Looking to the trees, Elle considered her next move.

"What guarantees do we have?" The second man, the one called Brian, said.

His brash companion hissed at him to shut up.

"The best I can give you is that I won't shoot you in the back, Brian. As long as we don't meet again, we're done," Elle said.

"What about the guys who hired us?"

"Hope you got partial payment upfront. If not, sorry about your luck. I suggest you disappear. Your employers had body bags waiting for you the moment you took the job."

"Don't be a pussy. She's just trying to mess with our heads. We can take her," the idiot said.

"Then have at it. Maybe we could take her, but I think she's right. We go to collect, and we're dead. If I'm not getting paid, then I don't give a shit if she lives or dies," Brian replied as he started to move away from her position.

Elle concentrated on the sound of him walking away, listening for indications that the idiot was using the movement as cover for his actions. He didn't move. But she did.

Elle didn't hesitate and crawled to a flanking position near the area where the idiot's voice had come from and closed the distance. She slowed as the sound of retreat faded and froze when her movements could no longer be masked, estimating that she was within a few feet of her target.

There was some rustling followed by footsteps moving away.

Suddenly the sound changed. The idiot turned, opened fire, and ran out toward where she had been, screaming, "Fuck you, bitch! I'm not falling for your shit!"

He was past Elle's new position in seconds. His form perfectly silhouetted through the NVGs by the muzzle flashes. She aimed and fired.

Silence fell again.

Elle sat for a few minutes in the quiet, waiting. Was she really alone now? The natural sounds of the forest had returned as though it hadn't just been a warzone. Trusting her gut and the instincts of the wildlife around her, she got moving. She had a small window to escape without a tail, and she needed to take it. Forgoing searching the corpses and leaving their gear, Elle got her bearings and started jogging.

CHAPTER 2

Monday, 2300: Near Strasburg, Virginia

Elle jogged for an hour before she saw lights through the trees. It was a rural, residential area. Not as nice as hers, but pleasant. Running to the closest house, she saw people moving around inside. *Damnit.* Looking around, she weighed her options. The houses were spread out, and it could take a while to find what she needed, but she had to get away clean. The chances of her being able to steal a vehicle without alerting the residents were non-existent. The car would be reported stolen before she turned off the road. Moving on, she headed north at a jog.

She could make out a house in the dark about half a mile ahead and made for it. A porchlight was on, but that was it. As she approached the house, she heard a dog bark inside. She stopped moving. It looked like the dog was home alone. She couldn't see any vehicles in the driveway, so she went to the barn. Pulling her lock pick, she made short work of the side door and opened it slowly. No alarm. Elle locked the door behind her and flipped on the light switch. An old, red Chevy pickup was parked in the barn.

Pulling the door open, she dropped down to get at the wires under the dash. Ripping them free, she found the leads she needed and stripped off their coating. When she closed the circuit, the engine coughed twice and then roared to life. Securing the wires, she shut off the lights, unlocked the barn doors, and pushed them open. She backed the truck out and closed the doors. With any luck, the homeowners wouldn't have a reason to go into the barn until tomorrow.

Elle inched the Chevy down the driveway to avoid making any noticeable tire impressions. Once on the street, she ran dark for a couple of miles before turning on the headlights. She felt exposed but would draw more eyes without them. Time to blend in. She continued north until she hit Interstate 66 and headed east toward Washington, D.C.

She drove for about an hour and decided it was time to stop for the night. It was very late, and she needed to clean and assess her wounds. It grated on her not to call for backup, but any calls she made would be traced. The chances of the evening's events going unnoticed were slim. Even out in the sticks, people tended to notice explosions and the sounds of gunfire. She couldn't risk being detained for questioning by anyone.

Elle wasn't CIA anymore. Even if she managed to avoid jail time, the fight with Tom Matthews in Rome was a major international incident—a diplomatic and political debacle that wasn't going away any time soon. Pictures of her and surveillance video of what had been a black-op played repeatedly over the last few days on every news network. It didn't matter that Tom had started the fight or leaked the video. The damage was done. It also didn't help that she'd embarrassed the Carabinieri when she escaped…the Italian government would want someone to pay.

Elle saw a sign for the Fairfax Marriott. It was close to the ramp to get her back on the highway fast if she needed to make a quick exit, and it was far enough outside the city to give her some anonymity. Finding parking in D.C. was damn near impossible. But, here, she could park the stolen truck and delay detection.

Sitting in the cab for a moment, she scanned the parking lot and the building. Several security cameras were visible on the corners of the hotel. Using the rearview mirror, she wiped at her face with the hem of her shirt to remove what was probably dirt and blood. Pulling a light jacket and ball cap out of her bag, she threw them on and tucked her hair up into the hat. Getting out of the truck, she walked into the hotel casually, angling away from the view of the cameras. Tom would have people looking for her, and she didn't intend on making this easy for him.

Walking into the lobby, she saw an older woman behind the counter. In the bright light of the hotel, Elle was grateful she had on dark-colored clothes. There were several places where the fabric had been torn, and she could make out multiple stains but hoped they wouldn't be identifiable from a distance.

Walking to the counter, Elle smiled. "Reservation for Smith."

The woman's name tag read Amy. She looked at Elle for a long moment before she started typing. "I'm sorry, ma'am, but I don't have a reservation under that name."

"You're kidding. My husband told me he made one. Could you check again?"

"No, Smith, sorry. But I do have rooms available."

"You're a lifesaver. I've been doing a nature challenge for the last couple of days, and it's been a disaster. I really just want to shower and sleep. Do you have anything that isn't near an elevator or icemaker?"

"Yes, ma'am."

"Fantastic. Could we have a room for three nights, Amy?"

"Two occupants?"

"Yes."

"ID and credit card, please."

Elle pulled out an ID for Sarah Smith and a credit card with the same name on it. She handed them to Amy.

She ran the card and gave both back to her once the transaction cleared. "Will you be needing two room keys?"

"I suppose we better. My husband's flight into Dulles was delayed, but he'll get here eventually."

"Do you need anything else, ma'am?"

"No, thank you."

The room was on the second floor, which wasn't ideal. If anyone came after her, they could reach the room easily and there wouldn't be much time to react, but she would make do. At least it was close to the emergency exit. She only intended to stay for tonight, anyway. Anyone running a hotel search would be looking for single women paying with cash. But they would expand their parameters and find her. By that time, she would be gone.

Inside the room, she locked the door and used a chair as a brace for an extra degree of security. Then she peeled off her clothes and dealt with the impact of tonight's ambush. It had been just shy of a week since everything went to shit in Italy, and if that wasn't enough, she was still healing from the wounds she took in Africa. Tonight's little adventure had done a number on her, too. She was covered in splotches of blood, both wet and dry. It was impossible to tell what was hers and what wasn't. Wadding up her old clothes, she threw them in the shower. She would need to get rid of them, but this way would make them less suspicious. Wet drew less curiosity than blood-stained.

Getting into the shower with the clothes, she turned on the hot water and let it work its magic. The water around her feet turned an ugly red as the blood slid off and drained from her clothes. Elle took her time washing her wounds, assessing each, and determining how to keep them from slowing her down. She was covered in bruises and abrasions, but she was okay for the most part. The bullet wound to her left shoulder had torn open some—her "souvenir" from the mission in Djibouti—but the bleeding was under control. She was lucky. Very lucky.

Minutes later, wrapping a towel around her and looking into the mirror, she could see why Amy appeared concerned. There were a couple of cuts along her cheekbone. They were raw and inflamed but not too deep.

Grabbing the first aid kit from her pack, she addressed the worst abrasions and applied antibiotic cream. Then she dressed and repacked her stuff. She needed to be ready to go at any time. Her stomach growled, and Elle couldn't remember when she'd last eaten. She raided the minibar and turned on the TV.

Breaking news lit up the screen, along with pictures of what was left of her house. Turning up the volume, Elle listened to the on-scene reporter. They didn't have much right now, but the story was already drawing massive interest. *"The woman outed as an assassin for the CIA…her secret country house explodes from a car bomb…bodies inside…."* It was a story straight out of Hollywood, and the media was drooling all over it. The extra attention wouldn't be doing her any favors. Her exposure as a spy was already front-page news, and she was supposed to lay low until the interest died away. This just fueled the frenzy. She was a little surprised that the reporter had managed to connect her to the house so soon, but Elle wasn't too interested in what they were saying. Instead, she focused on the images on the screen.

Bingo.

Just behind the reporter from CNN was a man in a dark-colored windbreaker. He was wearing a press lanyard but not asking any questions. He periodically took photos, but they were of the first responders. He was tracking people exposed to the scene. *Shit.* Tom wasn't done smearing her. Bribes would be paid, evidence would be lost, reports would be altered. Her adversary wanted her on the run from everyone. She had no doubt that the bodies in her house would somehow place her on the FBI's most-wanted list. And an "anonymous tip" would lead them to the bodies in the forest.

Grabbing her bag, she took out the wallet she'd taken from one of the hitmen inside her house. Flipping through it, she found cash, cards, and a driver's license. This guy was way out of his league—he was just a hired thug. Tom had planned for contingencies. Both hit teams had the numbers, firepower, and the element of surprise on their side and, even in failure, they could still assist him. He would be expecting her to reach out for help and go on the run. It was the smart play.

Why disappoint him?

Elle pocketed the cash from the wallet. Then, she went into the bathroom, wrung out her clothes—the water draining from them still had a faint, pink tint—and rolled up the rest of the contents of the wallet with them. Then she shoved them in a trash bag and set it by the door. Checking the hotel's amenities list, she found their laundry room. Next, she took her gun case out of the backpack and placed it in the closet, hidden inside the spare blankets. Closing the door, she yanked out a strand of hair and draped it across the door handle.

Putting on her jacket, she grabbed her backpack and the trash bag. The laundry room was on her floor, so she went to it first. There was a camera inside, so she threw the entire contents of the trash bag into the laundry. She purchased a single-use detergent pack from the vending machine against the wall and started the washing machine. Walking out, she went back to the front desk.

"Sorry to bother you again, Amy, but is there someplace open nearby that I could go and pick up a few items?" Lowering her voice, she added, "I'm afraid my time of the month came earlier than expected."

"Oh, dear. I'm sorry. Yes, there is, but we also carry some here for your convenience."

"Thank you, but I'm a little particular about my brands."

"I understand. There's a Walmart, open twenty-four hours, not too far from here."

After Amy gave her the directions, Elle was back on the road. She only had to jump on the highway for one exit before she was at the location. It was the middle of the night, but plenty of people were shopping. The hat shielded her from the myriad of cameras throughout the store. She went through the women's clothing section and grabbed neutral tones and items that could be worn layered. Next, she selected tennis shoes, a plain tan ball cap, and a reversible tote bag that went with her new look. Then it was onto the beauty aisle for travel-sized toiletries, makeup, and hair dye. Lastly, she hit electronics for two pay-as-you-go phones.

Back at the hotel, Elle kept up pretenses and went to the laundry room first. She pulled out the pants, gripping the stolen wallet under the material. Shaking her head as though the pants couldn't be saved, Elle balled them up and dumped them in the trash. She then placed the shirt in the dryer and returned to her room. After securing the door, she checked the hair on the closet door handle. It was still there. No one had tried to open the door while she was gone.

She spent several minutes pulling tags and getting her new items situated. Once that was all done, she set the alarm and laid down to sleep. She would need to be up again in a few hours, and that's when things were going to get fun.

CHAPTER 3

Tuesday, 0800: Fairfax, Virginia

While she'd managed to shake off the physical effects of her real-life nightmare, the lingering impacts from PTSD were creating a fair amount of anxiety. Last night hadn't done her any favors there. Elle listened with her ear to the door before leaving her room. Then, she used the stairs and the side exit to leave the hotel. She didn't want to chance Amy seeing her. Her image had changed so much from the night before, there would be questions. Now a brunette dressed in jeans, tennis shoes, and a light-green shirt, Elle looked more like a middle-class suburbanite than a dangerous fugitive. She wore makeup to mask the scratches and bruises and left her hair down. Elle could fade into the crowd anywhere, carrying her backpack, weapons case, and extra clothing in the big tote bag.

Outside the door, the taxi she ordered was waiting. Elle jumped in and had the driver take her to the Fairfax train station. From there, she took the train into Union Station, Washington, D.C. The building was alive, with people moving everywhere all at once. There were shops, bars, restaurants, and food vendors. Elle stood just outside the main concourse, where people were waiting for their trains, and pulled out her personal cell phone. Replacing the battery, she glanced around, waiting for the old gadget to power up. As soon as it was ready, she called her boss on his direct line. *Come and get me.*

"We've been trying to reach you, Anderson. Are you alright?"

Elle could hear the concern in Marcus Calloway's voice. That surprised her a little. Since being burned, Elle had assumed that Director Calloway's assurances that the CIA would do right by her were just kind words to ease her firing. "I'm alive, sir. I walked into an ambush. Two hit teams, six men each. They were well-armed but not well trained. My guess is they were local hires."

"The media is running with information supposedly coming from inside the investigation that you're linked to several drug cartels. They're saying you stole money and drugs, and the cartel came for you. By now, I doubt there's a law enforcement agency out there that isn't interested in finding you. Probably several criminal organizations, too."

"They had a backup plan in place for if I escaped the assault. I spotted a plant in the crowd around my house during some of the news coverage. He was marking everyone who had exposure to the scene. They were gathering intel so they would know how to influence the investigation their way."

"Who is 'they,' Ms. Anderson?"

"Thomas Matthews, and I think Mahmud Hussein, Number 3 from the original target list is here, too."

"That's quite a leap."

"They built in enough time before the attack started to try and mess with my head. The chair that Number 3 almost killed me in while I was in Iraq was waiting in my living room. And there was a greeting card on it that said *See you soon*. Only Tom Matthews could have found out what was happening to me and learn my next move. The chair had to have come from Number 3. And, yes, to answer your next question, I'm sure it was the same chair."

There was a long beat before Director Calloway said, "You need to come in now, Ms. Anderson. We will protect you and find Thomas Matthews."

"I can't do that, sir."

"Yes, you can. And you will," Calloway ordered.

"I believe your office is compromised. And I'm a burned spy. I would be running the gauntlet to be sidelined, or worse."

"Compromised? Explain."

"They knew where I was going to be and when. I have two houses, neither are listed under my name in public record. Debriefing could have lasted days, or I could have remained in custody, but they attacked within minutes of me walking in the door—they were tipped off. I didn't even know where I was going until you told me. So, the only way they got their information was through your office."

Silence.

"You need to clean house, sir. In the meantime, I'm going to finish this."

"That is absurd, Ms. Anderson. And not an option."

"It's the only option. I'm already being hunted by everyone, and you fired me."

"...So, why did you call?"

"You need to know what's happening. And if you're going to bait a trap, might as well make it useful."

"What the hell are you talking about?"

"I'm expecting company soon. Thanks for taking my call, sir. Please, look after my team." Hanging up, Elle glanced at her watch. That should have been plenty of time to get a trace on her location. She silenced the device, set up call forwarding to one of the burners, and then dumped the cell into a trash can. Moving away from the commuters on the platform, she walked toward the string of retail stores on the first floor and began window shopping in the literal sense.

She made a mental map of the various shops, noting all the reflective surfaces. They'd enhance her visual of the area where she dumped the cell phone without forcing her to stare at the trash can. She had just arrived at a jewelry kiosk when the burner phone rang.

That was fast.

Elle felt her anger surge but reigned it in. She wanted this. Answering the phone, she pretended Calloway was calling back. "Yes, sir?"

"I've missed you calling me 'sir.' It's good that you've remembered your place," Tom Matthews said.

Elle paused, drawing out the call while she watched for

the team she knew was on the way. They had to be close. The only advantage to calling her now was as a distraction. "What do you want, Tom?" she asked.

"I would think it's pretty obvious by now. I want you dead."

"Your obsession got old a long time ago. Perhaps, you should look into therapy or do us all a favor and put a bullet in your head."

"Always the smug, little bitch. I thought you would've learned some humility by now."

"You're one to talk. Your delusions and ego got you kicked out of the Agency. Now, look at you, burning connections, sticking your neck out, risking everything to go after an imaginary rival."

He laughed coldly. "I can do so much more now than I ever could at the Agency. You have no idea how many connections I have. Or what I have in mind for you."

Continuing to walk through the various shops, Elle put some distance between her and the target location while keeping eyes on it. "You're boasting to the wrong person. I couldn't care less about what you think you can do. We both know I'm better than you are. Your so-called connections and plans are worthless."

"We'll see about that."

She spotted two men moving through the crowd toward the trash can. Cops. "You can tell your boy Mahmud that I'm coming for you both."

"Oh, don't worry, Elle. I've made arrangements to ensure a special reunion. You got our gift? It was hard to give up my favorite piece. Such a shame it didn't get to see more use. But knowing that Mahmud showed you such a good time in that chair made each bloodstain so much more special. Although I did notice some extra staining on the seat. Did you piss yourself?"

The two cops paused at the trash can where Elle dumped the phone and started looking around. *Son of a bitch.* They were on his payroll. Being D.C. police explained how they got to her so fast. This was going to be interesting.

"I'll be sure to return your thoughtful gift with one of my own. It's been nice chatting with you." Hanging up, Elle shut off the phone and tucked it away. Watching the cops, she saw one take a call as they both looked around, searching the crowd. Tom or one of his lackeys just called to tell them they'd been made. The cops would start a grid search for her next. Stepping into a skincare boutique, Elle positioned herself close to two women being pitched by a saleswoman and pretended interest. Her appearance had changed, but was it enough? The cops would be looking for a woman alone, trying to keep a low profile. Time to make some friends.

Elle struck up a conversation with the women—Martha and her adult daughter, whose name she didn't catch. She kept the saleswoman engaged, drawing things out. Both women didn't appear to be in a hurry and chatted away politely. Meanwhile, she kept an eye on the movement of the cops. They were getting closer to her position as they systematically searched the area. *Let's see what you've got, boys.*

"Did you see that?" Elle asked the saleswoman.

"What?"

She pointed to a woman with reddish-brown hair moving through the shops in a hurry. "I think that woman just took a phone from that store."

"Where?" the saleswoman asked.

"Over there. Does it seem like she's avoiding those police officers? Should we tell them?" Elle looked at the salesperson expectantly.

Martha chimed in, "She does seem to be avoiding them. These days, it's best to be safe."

As the saleswoman stepped outside the store to flag down the police officers, Elle turned to the women. "I'm a little nervous. What if I forget to tell them something?"

"Don't worry, we'll stay with you," Martha replied.

"Thank you, I appreciate that." Elle watched the saleswoman talk to the police officers. Their faces went from polite indifference to intrigue once they got the description. The lead cop, the one who took the call, took off in the direction the saleswoman pointed and left his partner behind to gather more information. *Perfect.* He was the straphanger—involved, but only by association. And that made him the weaker link.

Returning to the store, the saleswoman gestured to Elle as the officer approached. "Ma'am, I'm Officer Bradley. Could you tell me what you saw?"

"Yes, sir." Elle smiled shyly. "I happened to be looking at that electronics store when I saw a woman pick up one of those pay-as-you-go phones by the counter. The guy behind the register was helping someone else, and it looked like she just cut open the package and put the phone in her pocket. It happened so fast I wasn't sure it had really happened. That's when I asked these ladies if they'd seen it, too."

Martha picked up the cue and said, "I didn't see her take the phone, but I did see her leaving quickly. It looked like she saw police and was avoiding you. That's why we wanted to make sure we reported it."

"You did the right thing, ma'am. Could you please describe the woman?"

"She was a young woman, skinny, with red hair. She was wearing jeans and a black jacket," Martha answered.

"Anything else?"

Martha looked at Elle and her daughter. They shook their heads. "No, sir. I'm afraid that's it."

"You've been very helpful, ladies, thank you." Bradley pulled a business card out of his shirt pocket and handed it to Martha. "If you think of anything else, please call." He turned away and used his radio to pass the description to his partner, and moved off to catch up.

"Well, that was quick," Martha said.

"Not sure what I expected. I guess I've watched too much TV," Elle said. A voice came over the loudspeakers announcing that a train to New York was boarding. "Oh, that's my train. I must have lost track of time. Sorry to run off, but it was so nice meeting you." As an afterthought, Elle added, "May I see that business card? Just in case I remember something else?"

"Of course. Here, keep it. Have a safe trip," Martha said as she handed over the card.

Elle walked toward the boarding area but headed for the exit in the opposite direction of Tom's pet cops as soon as she was out of sight. Plowing through the door, she went west until she found a Starbucks. Ducking inside, Elle watched the street while waiting in line to order. Just before reaching the counter, she pulled out the burner cell and pretended surprise and frustration. Once she got to the counter, she fiddled with the device a moment longer before smiling apologetically.

"Did your phone die?" the barista asked.

"Yeah. And I don't know why. It was fully charged this morning."

"That sucks. I'm sorry."

"Thanks. Could I get a Grande Caffè Mocha? And would it be possible to use your phone to call a cab?" Elle said.

"No problem, we can call one for you. What's the name?"

"Sarah. Thank you so much," Elle said. The barista wrote the name on the cup and then finished ringing up her order before stepping away to ask the manager to call a taxi.

Elle stood by the pick-up area with her back to the wall, eyeing the place in every direction. When they called out her drink, the manager let her know that a taxi was on the way. Elle sat and waited. Every car or pedestrian that passed was a potential surveillance unit, and Elle examined each in turn. She'd bought herself some time and distance, but it wouldn't last. Tom's people would start checking drills to reacquire her. She needed to be long gone by then.

Ten minutes passed before a yellow cab pulled in front of the Starbucks. Elle waved thanks to the Starbucks staff and left. Watching the driver, Elle didn't pick up any indications that the man was anything other than an employee dispatched on a call. The man barely looked at her when she got in, just set up his meter. And he matched the license picture on display.

"Where to?" he said, by way of greeting.

"Georgetown Neighborhood Library, please," Elle said.

The driver nodded and took off with only a quick glance at passing traffic. *Gotta love D.C. drivers.* As they drove, Elle sipped her coffee and watched her surroundings. She timed turning around to see if they were being followed to maximize her chances to spot tails, but not so much as to be noticeable. Surveillance could be hard to detect if the team was substantial in number and had enough resources at their disposal to allow her to be out of visual range for a period.

After about twenty minutes, they arrived at the library, and Elle felt confident that she had gotten away clean. Tom would be pissed. Smiling, she paid and got out. The old stone building looked just the way a library should. Inside, it was well lit with dark wooden shelves, black furniture, and, most importantly, public access computers. Elle went through the process of signing up for computer time and sat at an empty desk. She logged on and ran a Google search on Officer Greg Bradley. The abundance of publicly available information these days is a double-edged sword. We want freedom of information and transparency in business and government. But no one thinks twice about what impact that has on the individual: addresses, vehicles, schooling, court documents, birth records, marriage certificates, divorces, all publicly available.

Over the last couple of years, some jackasses had started aggregating publicly available information to try and extort money from people to help manage their "online image." It was all horseshit but scary to see how much they could put together. Put in some vague language to make it appear you're being linked to something nefarious, and people start shelling out money to make it stop.

Taking advantage of the practice, Elle searched for Greg Bradley and found a multitude of possible hits. She narrowed down the search using the man's description and profession to the most likely candidates. Before long, Elle had his home address and his wife's Facebook page. Getting onto the page confirmed she had the correct man. She scrolled through it for a while, gathering as many details about their lives as possible. Rookie cop, trying to start a family in the big city, likely money problems—this couldn't be more cliché. Elle tried to find any clues about Bradley's partner, but all she could find was a first name: Chris. At least it was a start.

Putting the address into Google Maps, Elle pulled up the location and used street view to see photos. It was a condo in McLean, Virginia. Not ideal but doable.

Game on.

CHAPTER 4

Tuesday, 1900: McLean, Virginia

It was just before sunset when Officer Greg Bradley got back to an apartment that was full of activity. The lights were on, the TV was playing some home improvement show, and the smell of food came from the kitchen.

And Elle was waiting for him.

"Hey, I'm home," Bradley called, closing the door behind him.

"Welcome home, dear," Elle said as she stepped into the room, gun drawn. "Don't make a sound, and don't move. It wouldn't be in Carrie's best interest."

He froze. Recognition made him tense more. "You. What have you done with my wife?"

"More to the point, what have you done to your wife? You got her involved with some very dangerous people. I hope you discussed your options before you decided to sell out."

"What are you talking about?" Bradley asked.

"Do you have any idea who's lining your pockets?"

"It's not like that! We're helping."

Elle laughed. "Is that what you tell yourself? That you're helping? Does that justify all the blood on your hands or the crimes you've aided?"

"You have no idea what you're talking about."

"Oh, that's cute. You are so naïve. No wonder they pulled you in. It was too easy. The trusting rookie with the new wife and financial problems. The pitch pretty much writes itself. I guess the real question is: Do you like being a paid lackey?"

"Fuck you."

"Not very original, but since nothing else about you seems to be, I should expect that. Put your gun on the table. Slowly. Then cuff yourself and sit on the floor." Once he complied, Elle said, "Okay, let's try something else. How do you think you're helping?"

"I don't have to tell you anything."

"You're right. But, apparently, you don't have a very good memory. I have your wife. You want to play games? So, let's play a game. Answers for Carrie's life.

"I want proof of life. Show Carrie to me," Bradley said.

Elle opened a closet door and yanked the woman out. She had been in a seated position, so she toppled onto her shoulder, bound and gagged. Tears were streaming down her face, and she was shaking.

"Oh my God, Carrie. I'm here, baby. It's going to be okay," Bradley said.

"You sure about that, Greg? You put her in this position. Put her at risk. For what? What was your price?"

"Go to hell!"

"And here I thought you were going to be reasonable. I guess you need a reminder of the stakes." Elle pointed the gun at Carrie. "She should at least hear how much you thought her life was worth. Don't you think?"

"Stop! Please, don't hurt her."

"Start talking, Greg. I'm running out of patience. Either you give me answers, or I start taking out my frustrations on her."

"Okay! Okay. Please. It started last week. My partner asked me if I wanted to make a little extra money off the clock freelancing for the CIA. I thought he was messing with me. But then he gave me two hundred dollars a day just to help him do surveillance on some big guy connected to …um, well, you, I guess."

Elle's stomach lurched. They were watching Tex, waiting for her to make contact. In addition to being her second in command, Agent Mike "Tex" Traviano was the closest thing to family she had. Would Tom try to grab him as leverage? What about the rest of her team? Julian could handle himself, but Eve and Jack were civilians and not trained to handle an assault. Elle pulled out the burner cell and typed a message to the one number she could think of that may not be compromised: *Matthews is going after my team. Tex first. Get them out now! Call me at this number when they're safe.*

"Keep talking."

"That was it until today. We were on patrol when Chris got the call that you were at Union Station. We went to assist with the manhunt."

"Who called?"

"What do you mean?"

"Who called Chris? Didn't you think it was strange he got a phone call and not a radio call? Did he report the tip after he got the information?"

Greg looked confused. "I assumed it was need-to-know."

"That's bullshit, and you don't even believe it. You went along with it because you wanted another payday."

Greg looked down at Carrie. She was no longer shaking, her attention on what her husband was divulging.

"I thought I was helping. The money was just a bonus."

Elle shook her head. "This is your one shot at getting clear of all this. Give me your partner and everything you know about the man you surveilled."

"Why?" Greg asked.

Elle didn't reply. She pulled out her knife and crouched over Carrie.

"No! No! What are you doing?"

"I warned you. Keep messing around, and Carrie suffers." Elle ran the blade across his wife's shoulder, slicing the fabric and causing Carrie to thrash and scream behind her gag.

Elle snatched her hair to stop the movement.

"I'll tell you everything! Just please don't hurt her!" Greg pleaded.

Elle kept the blade against Carrie's shoulder. "Don't move. Don't fight. Or we could have an accident. Start talking, Greg. And don't leave anything out."

***

Twenty minutes later, Elle was ready to move. Her hostages were bound and gagged side-by-side on the couch, scared but otherwise unharmed. They were mentally and emotionally beaten down but not as compliant as Elle had hoped. Time to shift tactics.

"If you want out of this with your lives, then pay close attention. The man who has been lining your pocket is the worst kind of traitor, and he's being hunted by the CIA. I exposed his crimes, and now he'll stop at nothing to kill me. Everyone on his payroll is after me—just like you. But not everyone on that payroll is innocent. He sent two hit squads to my home with explosives and automatic weapons. These people don't care about who gets caught in the crossfire, and they don't allow for loose ends. If you want to survive this, do exactly what I say. You're going to forget you ever saw me. I was never here. Tomorrow, you go to work just like always and act as though nothing has changed. This man has eyes everywhere. Don't draw attention to yourself. Do you understand?"

Greg nodded.

Elle detected hesitation, so she walked over and removed his gag.

"You're just going to let us go?"

"That all depends on you, Greg. If you've been truthful with me, then we're done here. You and Carrie can go on with your lives and be clear of all this soon—as long as you do as I say. But if you're lying or try to interfere, you won't survive the night."

Carrie squirmed and started crying again.

"My partner will know something is wrong. How am I supposed to hide something like this?" Greg asked.

"Your partner is in much deeper than you are and has more to lose. Chris will get a similar offer to what you're getting now. If he takes it, then he'll be focused on keeping up his own façade."

"And if he doesn't?"

"Do you really want the answer to that?" Elle asked.

"He's a cop! You can't do this!" Greg shouted.

Elle directed her comments to Carrie. "Your husband doesn't seem to understand what's happening here. Let me be perfectly clear. These people will kill you both. His so-called partner will be the first guy in line to do the job since he brought Greg into this. They will make Chris kill you both and cover it up. I want you to think hard about how well you really know Chris. Can you trust he will sacrifice himself to save you both? Or would he save his own skin? Because that will be the choice they give him."

Carrie was trying to speak.

Elle removed her gag.

Carrie's voice was a whisper when she asked, "How do we know we can trust you?"

"Good question. You don't. But since I haven't killed you both already, I'd say that speaks volumes. If either of you has watched the news lately, you know I have nothing to lose. I'm being hunted for crimes I didn't commit. So, the only thing stopping me from killing you both right now is that I don't want to. I'm not the bad guy."

"After what you've done, you expect us to believe that?" Greg asked.

"Other than being a little shaken up, there's not a mark on either of you. Carrie may have a couple of bumps from falling on the floor, and her shirt is ruined, but that's it."

They looked at each other and realized, if only on an intuitive level, that Elle was right.

Still, Greg was less convinced and asked, "Why? Why are we being spared?"

"I never believed you were dirty, just naïve. But I didn't have time to deal with breaking through the blue line. Your blind loyalty to the badge and your partner would have gotten a lot more people killed. I needed you to understand the stakes immediately. But if I'd been wrong about you, and you were in deeper than I thought, this would have gone very differently."

"So what happens now?" Carrie asked.

"That depends on you guys. What's your choice?"

Carrie looked at her husband, waiting for him to respond for them both.

Greg looked sick but was trying to put on a brave face. "I don't think we have much choice. We agree, or we die tonight."

"That's not an answer, Greg," Elle said. "But if it makes you feel better, you're right. So let me put it to you this way: Do you want your wife to die so you can protect a dirty cop?"

"No."

"Then your choice is simple. Follow my instructions, and you'll make it through this."

Greg nodded.

"Good. I'm going to borrow your truck for a little

while. The two of you will stay like this until I get back. It shouldn't be long, but I can't risk you going back on your word. When I return, I'll release you both, and, with any luck, we'll never see each other again."

"You can't leave us like this."

"Would you prefer I put you in the truck bed and take you along?"

Greg shook his head and started to reply, but Elle cut him off. "You don't want to be a part of this any more than you already are."

"How did you know what I was about to—"

"You don't exactly have a poker face."

"If Chris is dirty, I should be part of the takedown. He's my partner. I need to be sure."

"Noble. I can appreciate your position. But stay with your wife. There's a good chance someone is going to die tonight. You don't want to be involved with that, and you definitely don't want it to be you. Then no one will be here for Carrie. If you understand one thing, let it be this: This is bigger than you."

Elle sympathized with the guy. Green as he was; Greg Bradley seemed to be one of the good ones under all the ignorance. Hopefully, he'd make it through this and use the experience to become a better cop.

Elle was weighing her next move when her phone rang. "Are they safe?" she asked.

The familiar voice of Doctor Patrick Wise, her handler, said, "Your team is on the way to HQ now. I didn't want to waste time, so I alerted Tex and Chief Saunders directly. The two of them were able to extract themselves, and they pulled Eve and Jack out moments ago. Tex said they identified surveillance at each location. The exception being at Chief Saunders' residence. I know he's a new addition and not likely a target, but I didn't want to risk leaving him out." Wise may be a CIA psychologist, but he was more operator than shrink as a former Navy SEAL. Old habits die hard, and there wasn't anyone more equipped to work with operatives. While Elle only ever took her orders from Director Calloway, Wise was the man who had helped her get back in the field. And, now, he had saved her team. She owed him everything.

Elle felt her chest relax. "Thank you. I never thought I'd use the phone number you gave me after I was fired, but I'm glad you made me take it. When my team gets to headquarters, tell Tex to go to the location where we first met, tonight, same time."

"Why not just have him call you when he arrives?"

"This is the second time I've been in contact with you on this line, and I know there's a mole in HQ. I can't risk using it more right now—and I need to keep this call short."

"This is a burner cell. It's unlikely that it's compromised. So, I would say you're just being paranoid, but I know better. I'll set up another means for you to contact me and pass it to Tex, just in case."

"Thank you. I'll never forget it."

"You're better than Thomas Matthews—just stay in control. Don't let him push your buttons. We need you."

The call disconnected, and Wise was gone.

A wave of emotion rolled through her, and Elle worked

to bury it—her hostages were watching. Wise would have insisted she allow herself to feel everything. It was part of her recovery regimen from severe trauma. But he had also caveated that she could choose when to allow herself to break down. Now was not the time.

Reining in her feelings, she threw herself back into the fray. Elle grabbed Greg's service pistol from the table and the badge she'd pulled from his belt, holding them where he could see, she said, "I'm taking these as insurance. If all goes well, they'll be back in your possession before your next shift. Get any crazy ideas about intervening or going back on your word, and I'll make sure this badge and gun are tied to multiple felonies. And then gift-wrapped for Internal Affairs. Am I clear?"

"We won't say anything," Carrie said without hesitation.

"Greg? Do we have an understanding?" Elle could see that he was struggling with some internal debate. "I want to hear you say it, Greg."

"I won't say or do anything...but please, don't kill my partner."

"That's up to him. If both of you stay calm, I'll leave the gags off. No screaming after I leave. You should have plenty to discuss while I'm gone. Besides, I wouldn't want for us to get this far only to have to kill you later." Backing away, she was out the door and on the run again.

Elle used the key fob to confirm which truck in the lot was Greg's—the lights flashed on the late model Chevy Silverado. *Nice truck but shit for anything clandestine.* She'd have to make do. Jumping behind the wheel, she typed in the address of her next target into the navigation system. It was already there. Studying the surrounding area on the map, it appeared to be an apartment in the part of Alexandria known as Old Town. Not good. Lots of people, and lots of security. But it also told her how deep Officer Chris Stokes was. While it wasn't so extravagant to draw immediate attention, the chances of a patrol officer being able to afford a place in Old Town were slim. He either got one hell of a deal, or his supplemental income was really enhancing his lifestyle.

The late-night dinner crowd would be out, and it would take her at least thirty minutes to get to the apartment. Stepping on the gas, Elle got moving. As she drove, an idea formed, and she found herself smiling. Stokes would never see it coming.

CHAPTER 5

Tuesday, 2000: Alexandria, Virginia

Old Town was alive. Cars were cruising through the streets as pedestrians strolled to and from the various bars and restaurants. It was so much easier to get where you wanted to go on foot since parking was at a premium. Even on a weeknight, everyone was well dressed. Whether coming from work or dressing to socialize, most people in this area wanted to be seen. Elle's casual outfit may have stood out under normal circumstances, but it was doubtful anyone would pay her much attention once she "accessorized."

She left the truck in a paid parking garage and started walking. Officer Chris Stokes' residence was just off the main thoroughfare. Beautifully maintained, it had to cost a fortune to live here. Stopping in the first place she saw that had what she needed, Elle ordered a cheese pizza to-go. The restaurant had merchandise, so she purchased a ball cap with their logo on it. Quick and easy. Elle pulled the bill down as she moved across the street and walked right up to the front door of her target's apartment building.

The panel by the door had call buttons for each unit and a small camera. Elle pushed the button for his apartment and then pulled out the burner phone to act as though she was texting. A male voice crackled through the intercom. "Think you got the wrong number. I didn't order any pizza."

Elle acted bored. "This is the number they gave me. Got 20 bucks to deliver it. I don't care who actually gets it. Figured it was a gift. If you don't want it, give it to someone else."

"Who sent it?"

"It's probably in the card," Elle said.

"There's a card?"

"Uh, yeah. So, do you want it or not?"

The door buzzed, and Elle grabbed the handle and walked in. The hallway was well lit and updated with modern décor. The apartment she was looking for was on the third floor, so she took the elevator. On the way up, she pulled her pistol from the holster, palmed it, and balanced the pizza on top, holding the box at waist level. Arriving on the third floor, she moved toward the front of the building. Chris Stokes had a street view from his place.

He opened the door just as she stopped in front of it. Staying in role, Elle held the pizza box out. "Here you go."

"Thanks." The second his hands gripped the sides of the box, Elle made her move. Her right hand wrapped around the pistol grip as she pushed the barrel into his gut in one fluid movement.

His eyes widened, and he looked ready for action.

"You'd be dead, and I'd be gone before anyone ever got to you. Think very carefully about your next move, Stokes."

"What do you want?"

"To talk. Now back into your apartment. No sudden moves or this will be a very short conversation."

He backed into the main living area and froze.

From the look of the place, he was a bachelor, but Elle asked, anyway, "Are you alone?"

"Yes."

"This would not be a good time for any surprises. I'm a little on edge these days, so if I hear any unexpected noises, I may shoot first and ask questions later."

"No one's here, and I'm not looking for any trouble."

"Funny. Pretty sure you've been looking for it all day. How much is Thomas Matthews paying you?"

The color drained from his face. For a moment, Elle thought he might try to bolt.

"You're her. Elle Anderson."

"Answer my question, Stokes."

"Look, I don't know what you think you—"

Elle raised her SIG P229 to his head, manually cocking the hammer, going from double action to single.

"Okay, okay, wait! It's just a job, alright! I don't know anything, and I don't care. Not as long as I get paid."

He's a terrible liar. "How does it work?"

"I get a phone call or a text message with instructions. Then, when it's done, money gets wired to my account."

"Show me," Elle demanded. "No sudden movements. I want to see your hands at all times."

Stokes moved to the table by his couch and grabbed a cell phone. He unlocked the screen and held it as if getting ready to hand it to her. Elle knew the attack was coming before he even twitched a muscle. When he lunged, she was already on the move, kicking one of the barstools directly into his path. It impacted his knees, ending his attempted assault before it even got started. Stokes went crashing to the ground on top of the barstool. He cried out in pain.

"Next time, it's a bullet." Elle picked up the phone he'd dropped while staying trained on her target. It was still unlocked, so she disabled the security features. Moving to the arm of the couch, she sat down as if she owned the place.

Stokes started to push himself up.

"Don't fucking move."

"I won't try anything again. I swear. Just please let me sit up. This hurts."

"Good. If it hurts, it should keep you focused. I may have all I need from your phone now, so I have no patience for bullshit. Last warning, stay down."

Stokes stopped moving, but Elle could identify the emotions crossing his face. He was going to be stupid, sooner or later. "Let's talk about the people who hold your leash and line your pockets. Who do you report to?"

"I don't know."

"Really? Okay, so I guess we're done here." Elle stood and aimed.

"They'll kill me!"

"What do you think I'm going to do if you don't give me what I want?"

"You'll never get away with it."

Elle moved toward a duffel bag that caught her eye. "Is that your final answer?"

Stokes was watching her every move, looking for an opening.

She let him think he had one. Holstering her gun, she reached into the duffel and wrapped her hand around the handle of a softball bat. She paused for just a moment. He jumped up and rushed her, expecting her to stand and swing the bat. She didn't. Staying low, she thrust the end of the bat into his groin. The impact drove the wind out of him long enough for Elle to bring the bat parallel to the ground and thrust upward using the force of both her arms and legs. The center of the bat collided with his chin. He crumpled to the ground.

Blood trickled from where his head hit the floor and from the corner of his mouth. Checking for a pulse, Elle confirmed he was alive but unconscious. Working fast, she bound his hands and feet with the athletic tape from the duffel bag. Once he was secured, she scrolled through the phone until she found the app for his bank. It was locked with biometrics. Using Chris's finger, she unlocked it and did a cursory search of his financials. Nothing seemed out of place. He must be getting paid in cash.

Elle systematically made her way through the apartment, searching for a safe. Walking into his bedroom, she found a large gun safe inside the closet. Too obvious. Continuing the search, she covered the rest of the room.

Elle stepped around the corner of the bed, and that's when she heard a creak. She stopped and looked at the floor, shifting her weight to confirm the loose board. Ripping back the rug, she could make out cuts in several planks and a small fingerhold. Old school, but effective. Lifting the boards, Elle found a second safe. Both had biometric locks—Stokes wanted to keep his secrets.

He's in too deep to be convinced to cooperate, and I'm not dragging his sorry ass back here. Walking to the kitchen, Elle pulled some ice out of the freezer, then grabbed a dish towel and a large knife.

***

Ten minutes later, Elle was sitting back on the arm of the couch, sifting through Stokes' text messages and calls. She had a trail to the next link in the chain, but she still needed information. A groan told her the time for answers was finally here. "Wake-y, wake-y. You owe me some answers."

He was lying on his side with his arms bound behind his back. His right arm had to be numb, and he wiggled to try and move into a better position. It was useless. "Fuck you," Stokes slurred.

"No thanks. What you can do is tell me what you know about your contact. Thomas Matthews may have recruited you, but it looks like you get your orders from one of his minions. There's no name in your phone, but I have the number and the messages you neglected to erase today. I'll get to them, one way or the other. The easier you make that for me, the nicer I'll be to you."

"I'm not going to tell you shit." Stokes spit bloody saliva at her. Elle sat motionless as it landed by her foot.

"Well, if you're not going to be reasonable, then I suppose I'll just keep my gift," Elle said.

"You don't have anything I want."

"Are you sure?"

Elle could see the fog lifting and doubt creep in. She picked up a small plastic storage container with ice in it. The contents were bloody. Reaching in, she pulled out a finger. "I was going to return this to you with enough time for it to be reattached. But, since you don't want it, I'll just go ahead and toss it."

The color drained from his face, and his eyes and mouth widened in shock. He couldn't see his hands, but Elle knew he'd be able to feel the place where the missing digit should be with the other hand. Stokes started panicking like crazy.

"No screaming, Stokes. Wouldn't want to make things worse for yourself."

"You fucking bitch!"

"I'm going to make this offer once. Do what I say, answer all my questions, and you'll live. I'll even make sure you get to an ER in time to get your finger reattached. If you don't, I walk out of here right now and leave you to fend for yourself. How do you think this will go over with your watch commander at the precinct? Or with Tom Matthews?"

"I'm not who you think I am! You're making a mistake!"

"You're half right. You aren't who I thought you were. You're worse." Elle showed him the contents of the duffel bag at her feet; it was full of money, with about a dozen IDs serving as the cherry on top. None were his.

His eyes widened with recognition before he returned to playing the victim. "It's not my fault. If I don't do what they ask, I'm a dead man," he pleaded.

Elle scooped up the IDs and tossed them on the couch. "Every one of these belongs to a young woman. Some are foreign, but most are U.S. citizens. You're a trafficker. Or do you prefer to be called a pimp? Is this money your purse? Is that how Tom was able to buy a cop so easily? He already knew how dirty you were?"

"Those girls would be dead if it wasn't for me. They need me."

The mission was already personal—but, now, emotions raging, her own hostage situation surfaced, blurring her focus. Elle could smell the basement in Iraq, feel the bite of the ropes at her wrists. Taste the blood in her mouth. Feel the hand of her abuser across her cheek. "Choose your next words very carefully, Stokes."

"Please. Let me go. I can help you."

"I want your connection to Tom Matthews, the location of the so-called stable where these girls are, and names of everybody else involved. Now."

"I can't—"

Elle launched off the arm of the couch for added momentum and kicked Stokes square in the gut. His breath rushed out so fast he gagged. As he coughed, she shoved a rag into his mouth, disrupting his involuntary attempts to catch his breath. He started thrashing on the floor in panic. Elle snatched his hair and placed the kitchen knife against his cheekbone. His eyes found hers, and his nostrils flared and contracted from the effort to take in enough air. "That was your last chance. I'm not asking again."

Increasing the pressure on the blade, she cut into his cheek, drawing the knife back to his hairline. He shrieked behind the gag. Even muffled, his pain was evident. Blood trickled over the bridge of his nose, dripping onto the floor. "How's it feel to be helpless? Marked as someone's bitch? Wonder what kind of price I could get for you? Doesn't matter how I mark up your face. I'm sure the kind of people who would pay won't mind the scars."

The noises coming from Stokes took on a different pitch and rhythm. He was begging for his life. "I'm going to remove that gag. Once. Only once. If I don't hear what I want to hear, my face will be the last thing you ever see. Do you understand?"

He nodded.

Elle pulled the gag out, ready for any attempts to scream.

"The girls are in an apartment building north of D.C." He paused to catch his breath. "We bring them to a penthouse near Dulles whenever we need to do business."

"Keep talking."

"There's two guards most of the time. Unless we bring in new…girls."

"How many bottoms do you have inside helping you?"

"How do you know—"

Elle covered his mouth with the gag and stabbed him in the leg. She could feel the vibration of his scream run through her hand and up her arm. "I'm out of patience. Answer my fucking questions."

"Okay, okay, please! Three girls help us keep the others in line. They're in the first room on each floor."

Elle pulled up the contact who had called while Stokes was hunting her at Union Station. "Who is this?"

"His name is Jonathan Nash, ex-Green Beret."

"Will he be at the apartment building with the girls?"

Stokes hesitated, so Elle put pressure on the blade, the tip still inside his leg.

"Stop! Yes, he stays there whenever he's in town."

"Details, Stokes. I want to know everything about the location and this Jonathan Nash. Let me be clear. Every time you stop talking, I'm going to twist this blade. Every time you try to be clever, I'm going to twist the blade. And if you hold anything back, I'm going to slit your throat."

***

Stokes eventually passed out from pain and blood loss, but Elle had enough to move on. Grabbing the bag with the cash, Elle piled in the guns and ammunition she'd taken from the weapons safe—*this asshole won't be needing them anytime soon.* Glancing at the limp body on the floor, she weighed her options. Killing a cop, even a dirty one, was going to complicate things even more. It was one thing to be a wanted fugitive, another to be labeled a cop killer.

If she just walked away, he might survive. But that may also give him time to find a way to derail her plans. *How do I neutralize him without ending his life or alerting Tom?* She had one option. Going back to the safe in the bedroom floor, she pulled out what she assumed was heroin. Stokes and the other traffickers probably used it to force cooperation from their victims. She was more than happy to return the favor.

Elle had never handled the drug before. She had to rely on what she'd heard. She took a small amount—hoping it was enough to have an effect but not enough to kill him—

and sprinkled it in the open wound on his leg. It would get in his bloodstream, sure enough, though what the impact would be was anybody's guess. Hopefully, enough to make anything he said or did suspect and buy her some time.

Moving through the apartment, she wiped every surface she'd touched and then left traces of the drug around the open floor safe with the stolen IDs back inside. Standing with her back to the front door, she surveyed the scene. Anyone walking in would assume Stokes had been tortured into giving up the location of his drug stash. Elle almost wished she could watch Stokes struggle to defend himself when further investigation leads his colleagues to the trafficking victims. Shouldering the bag of money and weapons, Elle walked out, leaving his door ajar. Taking the stairs, she returned to the first floor. On her way out of the main entrance, she pulled the fire alarm.

A high-pitched, oscillating squeal followed her out the door. Pulling off the ball cap and shaking out her hair, she walked down the street as if she didn't have a care in the world. She was a couple of blocks away when she heard the approaching sirens. Pulling out Stokes' phone, she used the map function to locate her next target: twenty minutes away and in the suburbs. This was not going to be easy.

She checked her watch. Thirty minutes until she was to meet with Tex. Every minute she wasted going after Jonathan Nash increased the chances of him slipping through her fingers. If Stokes managed to warn Nash, she'd never get to Tom before he got to her. But she could use some backup for this next part. There were too many variables to feel comfortable about the odds.

Elle made it back to the truck without incident. Throwing the duffel in the back seat, she sat behind the wheel, wargaming out her options. There was only one play.

CHAPTER 6

Tuesday, 2130: Washington, D.C.

Elle was fortunate enough to find a parking spot within walking distance of the Lucky Bar. She sat and watched traffic for a while before hopping out of the Silverado. Nothing seemed out of the ordinary, but she refused to let her guard down. Walking toward the building, Elle recommitted to her chosen course of action. She'd link up with Tex and, with his help, would take out the traffickers and seize her next target.

The delay was eating at her, but this was the right move. Tex wouldn't need any convincing once he knew the stakes. Walking through the glass doors, Elle entered the sports bar. For being in the heart of D.C., it was a pretty low-key establishment. It was late, so most of the screens were airing highlights. And it wasn't busy, so she snagged a spot at the end of the bar, where she could keep an eye on the entrance. Then, she ordered a beer and waited. Normally, she would have staked out the location and watched whomever she was meeting enter first. That way, she could be sure they weren't being followed. But these were not normal times. At precisely 2130, after ten minutes of no activity, the door opened.

Chief Julian Saunders, Navy SEAL and newest member of her team, walked in. Alone.

Elle's heart rate skyrocketed. *Breathe.* Julian didn't approach her position, though she was certain he knew where she was sitting. Instead, walking straight to the bartender, he placed an order and waited. The bartender returned with two bottles. Julian paid, grabbed the bottles by the neck, and walked over.

"Tex told me not to let you drink your usual piss water. So, I got you a real beer." Julian gave her a Sam Adams.

Elle's tension eased a little. Tex sent Julian. That was the only way he could have known the details about their beer debate. Still... "Where is Tex?"

"We assumed he would get tailed the second he tried to leave HQ. So, Tex drew surveillance while I came to link up with you. He's leaving chalk marks in different spots to make it look like he's signaling you. Then he's going to grab some food. That should keep the surveillance team spinning their wheels for a while. They're not likely to try and grab him if they think he's going to lead them to you. Once he's done eating, he's going to head back to HQ."

It was a solid tactic, but Elle was irritated that Tex wasn't here. Elle reached into her pocket and pulled out the phone she'd taken from Stokes. "I need Jack and Eve to tear this thing apart and get me any details they can about an ex-Green Beret named Jonathan Nash."

"That name sounds familiar. Who is he?" Julian asked as he put the phone in his pocket.

"The next wrung on the ladder to Thomas Matthews," Elle said as she started to get up.

Julian placed a hand on her arm. "Elle, please. Talk to me."

Elle paused a moment. She could feel the warmth of his skin through her sleeve. Though Elle was hard-pressed to accept it, the connection between them was palpable. Her struggle with severe post-traumatic stress had caused her to lose control. She'd used him, both personally and professionally, and then pushed him away. She'd hid behind the needs of their mission. He deserved better.

"I'm sorry, Julian," she managed to say. "For everything. I'm glad you're safe now, but I put you all through hell. It's time for me to finish this."

"You need to drop the lone wolf act. I know the risks and what you're about. I'm here. Ready to jump back into the fire with you."

Her chest tightened. Julian could trigger her emotions like no one else. "It's going to be ugly. And illegal. The CIA has no jurisdiction stateside. Calloway can't protect you from the fallout if we're caught."

"Sounds like a typical Saturday night. Where are we going?"

"Nash is a human trafficker. He's going down, hard, and so is everyone involved. I have the location where he keeps the girls."

Julian stood, determination evident, as he held out his hand. "What are we waiting for?"

Smiling, she took it. They left the bar looking like a couple on a date. As they walked to the truck, Elle asked,

"Are you armed?"

"A pistol at the small of my back and a pocketknife. I was in a bit of a hurry and wasn't planning on a siege when I left the house tonight."

"Lucky for you, I was."

When they got to the truck, Elle jumped behind the wheel and pulled up the target location on the GPS. "The apartment building is here. It's a lower-class area just north of D.C., but it's a residential neighborhood. It'll be hard to get in there without being noticed at this time of night."

"That leaves us two options: stealth or shock and awe," Julian said.

"It'll be locked down, so stealth won't help us get through the doors. And I have no doubt they'll use human shields, so a full assault will go south fast. How about something in between?"

"I'm all ears."

Elle reached into the glove compartment and pulled out Officer Bradley's badge and service weapon. She placed both on her belt, then grabbed a police windbreaker out of the duffel, which she'd also taken from his apartment. Tossing it to Julian, she smiled. "Time to canvass the neighborhood, Officer Saunders."

"Ballsy. But it should get them to open the door to try and talk their way out of the situation."

"They know one of their own is a cop. This won't be seen as a threat, just an inconvenience. They'll look to pacify and name drop. Once the door is open, we'll have a couple of minutes max to position ourselves to neutralize the traffickers. We can expect at least two guards in addition to

Nash. And the first woman on each of the three floors is complicit, so they may fight us or try to aid the guards."

"Are you thinking Stockholm syndrome?"

"For some, maybe. For others, it could be shame or fear. Drugs could be a factor. They may not be able to process what's happening or think it's a trick. The best thing we can do is keep them secured so they don't get hurt or call in the cavalry."

"What do we do with Nash?"

"I want him alive. He's coming with us."

"Then what? Where to?" Julian asked.

"I'm still working on that part. Our options may be pretty limited depending on what kind of shape he's in. I'll make the call once we have him."

Looking at the weapons inside the duffel bag, Julian pulled out a Glock and several magazines. He smiled. "Well, I've worked with less. Let's do this."

They rode in silence, mentally preparing for what was coming. Elle parked the truck at the end of the target block. Grabbing a notebook from the backseat, she handed it to Julian. "Just follow my lead. We're going to make our way down this side of the street first. Any lookouts the traffickers posted have already keyed on us. We want them to see us treating this as a routine canvass. I'm guessing by the time we're halfway down the block, word will have gotten back to our target about why we're here. They'll either decide to handle it on their own or call in re-enforcements."

"What kind of re-enforcements?"

"Dirty cop."

"Isn't that going to be a problem?"

"Nope. He's in no shape to help. Besides, his phone is in your pocket."

Julian just shook his head. "Feels like I need a beer for that story."

They were on the opposite end of the street from the target apartment building. This part was lined with townhomes. They played out the same scenario at each residence, telling the occupant they were looking for anyone with information about an armed robbery that occurred on the next block. They treated it as though they were just following basic procedure and broke away at the first negative response.

Most of the people they talked to reacted how she expected anyone roused by the police at night would—confused, concerned, irritated. Elle was starting to think that maybe she'd overestimated the amount of security Nash would have—until they got to the last townhome. It was across from the target building and seemed to be in better shape than the others. As they made their way up to the front door, movement in front of a second-floor window caught her attention. The hair on the back of her neck stood on end.

"We're being watched. Second floor," Julian said under his breath.

"I see it. Keep acting like this is all just routine."

Elle knocked on the door. Something told her she wasn't going to like what was about to happen. When the door opened, it took a lot of effort not to react. *Fucking bastards.* A young girl in a nightgown answered. She couldn't have been more than sixteen.

"Hi. Sorry to disturb you so late. Are your parents' home?"

"No. They're at work. Is something wrong?"

"There was a robbery nearby. We're following up on a possible lead and asking everyone in the neighborhood if they have seen a white, late-model Honda Civic in the area."

"Sorry, I can't help you."

"Thanks for your time. Have a good night."

Turning away, Elle caught the troubled look in Julian's eyes.

"We knew this was going to be a long shot. So, let's just finish this street and call it for the night," Elle said loud enough to be heard through the door.

Julian nodded. "The sooner, the better. I'm ready whenever you are."

Walking away from the house, with her voice low, she added, "They should be calling their friends in the target building now. If they bought it, their guard will be down. First, we need to get inside without setting off any alarms. Then we need to be fast."

"What about the girl we just saw?"

"We'll go back for her after we secure the target."

"Once the shooting starts, they could run and take her with them," Julian said.

"They might. Or they may use her against us. She's been seasoned. They trusted that she would stick to the script and not betray them. She's going to do whatever they tell her to do. They could use her as a bargaining chip or put a gun in her hand and force us to kill her. We have to be ready for the probability that we're not going to be able to save everyone, Julian."

Julian tried not to show any emotion, but Elle saw the muscles constrict as he clenched his jaw. “Ready to do this on your mark, Elle.”

A chill ran through Elle. From the tone, he was out for blood. “Keep your game face on. We still need to get inside.”

The apartment building was older, but the entryway had been updated with a new door and intercom system. Elle skimmed the names…all generic. Then, selecting the very first apartment, she pressed the button. After a brief pause, she heard a man ask, “Can I help you?”

“Good evening, sir. I’m Officer Bradley with DCPD. We’re canvassing the neighborhood to see if anyone may have any information that could assist us regarding a robbery that occurred earlier this evening. Could you please let us in? This shouldn’t take long.”

“Uh, okay, give me a minute. I’ll come out to you.”

A minute later, through the glass entryway, Elle could see a door open in the hallway. The man walking toward her screamed underling: skinny, with greasy slicked-back hair, wearing all black and expensive jewelry. Smiling patiently, Elle nodded at the man putting her hand on the door handle as if waiting for entry.

“Sorry, but can I see your badge?”

“Of course.” Elle held up Officer Bradley’s badge, then launched into her questions before he had the chance to ask to see Julian’s badge.

“Sir, have you heard anything about a home invasion in the area?”

“No, sorry.”

"Have you seen a late-model, white Honda Civic in the neighborhood?

"Not that I can think of."

"Appreciate your time, sir. Unfortunately, I've run out of business cards, but I can leave my number with you in case you think of anything. Could you please let us in so we can canvass your neighbors too?"

Elle saw a flicker of unease cross the minion's face, but he didn't have much choice. If he said no, it would be suspicious. "Uh, sure. Sorry, but some of my neighbors aren't very social."

"We know it's late, but we don't intend to be here long."

The man's smile was fake, but he opened the door. Elle walked in without hesitation so that he couldn't change his mind. Julian followed close behind. "Appreciate your cooperation. We'll be done as soon as we can. Is there an elevator? We'll start on the third floor and work our way back down to make this go faster."

The minion's voice cracked when he answered. "The elevator is busted, but the stairs are at the end of the hall."

They would have put the newest acquisitions on the third floor, less chance for them to escape. They also may be less seasoned than the rest, increasing the chances for something to go wrong for the traffickers. This was dangerous ground. Forcing Elle and Julian to take the stairs was a way to track their movements. Not to mention, stairwells were not someplace you wanted to be in a firefight. Whoever had the high ground had the advantage.

Walking through the hall, Elle made a note of the layout. She listened for any sounds that could help her identify what might be happening behind closed doors. There were six apartments on this level, with likely the same layout on the other floors. She could hear TVs playing but no conversation. Eyes were on them. She could feel it.

In the stairwell, Elle noticed cameras and high-security locks on the doors. "Damn. Today was leg day. Really wish that elevator was working."

Julian took her cue and kept the conversation light. "You're getting soft. Maybe you ought to switch over to yoga?"

Their banter continued until they hit the third floor. As soon as they made the landing, a woman approached. She acted startled, but she wasn't a very good actress.

"Oh! Um, sorry, I was just leaving. Is there something I can help you with, officers?"

"Yes, ma'am. We're canvassing the area looking for anyone who may have any information about a robbery. Do you have a moment to answer a few questions?" Elle said.

"I don't know anything about a robbery. Sorry. Hope you catch them," She said with an air of finality.

"Okay, well, how about a white, older Honda Civic?"

"Nope. Sorry."

"Thank you for your time, ma'am." Elle started to walk past her, but the woman stopped her.

"None of the other apartments are occupied up here right now."

"Must be nice having the floor all to yourself. Do you live with anyone?"

"My boyfriend, but he's not home right now."

"Alright, guess we can move on. Oh, I'm out of business cards, but I can leave you my information if you have a piece of paper and a pen. That way, if your boyfriend knows anything that could be of assistance, he can call me."

"I'm sure he doesn't know anything. He doesn't go out much."

"But he may have seen or heard something helpful. It's standard procedure. I'll give you my contact info, and we'll be on our way," Elle said. Then, turning to Julian, she added, "I'm going to finish up here. Why don't you go ahead and head down to the next floor? Be quick. Then meet me on the main level. It's time to call it." Julian nodded, and he left.

Elle smiled at the woman expectantly.

She nodded, turned back toward her door, unlocked it, and went inside. Elle waited in the hall and marked time in her head. Estimating how long it would take Julian to make it to the first apartment on the second floor and get them to open the door.

Now.

The door of the apartment had just started to open back up when Elle made her move. She kicked it open the rest of the way and drew her pistol in one fluid movement. The door slammed into the woman, knocking her off her feet. A guard was standing to the side of the door, with a shotgun in his hands. Elle put a bullet in his head and then shot the woman in both legs. She crumpled into a ball screaming, but Elle didn't pause to see what happened next. Spinning around, she hit the stairs at a run. The echo of gunshots coming from the next floor quickened her pace.

At the second-floor landing, the door opened, and Julian burst through. His demeanor was all business. Elle allowed herself a fraction of a second to appreciate having him with her before continuing down. Julian fell in behind her as they sprinted down to the main floor. Stopping at the bottom of the stairs, Elle kicked open the door. The wood on the frame exploded in two places, sending splinters everywhere. Dropping to a knee, she leaned out just enough to view the hallway and see two men moving toward them with shotguns. She opened fire on both, hitting them repeatedly in the chest. They staggered and fell forward. "Move!"

"Moving," Julian responded as he navigated around her and started down the hall.

Elle fell in behind him, staggering her field of fire and watching their six. A door opened at the end of the hall, and the minion popped out, a gilded gun in his hand. Clearly, it was a showpiece and not something he ever thought to use. Although he started to raise the gun, holding it sideways, he never completed the move. Julian put two rounds through his forehead without breaking stride.

"Don't stop," Elle ordered as they approached the open apartment door.

Julian rushed through it, staying left, with Elle behind him going right. The room was empty, but Elle's internal warning system shrieked at her. "Cover!" she warned, just as an object came flying into the room from the hallway. The room exploded with the intense light and noise of the concussion grenade.

Disoriented, Elle was a second slower than her opponent. He was on her in an instant, knocking away her gun and seizing her by the throat. He pulled her up, and she felt the barrel of his gun under her chin. Her vision cleared enough to see Julian with his weapon trained on them. The hot breath on the back of her neck told her that this guy wasn't stupid. He wasn't holding his "hostage" Hollywood-style, that was for sure. He was using his human shield effectively, keeping as much of himself behind her as possible.

"Clever, bitch. You must be the one he's looking for. Didn't expect you to come knocking on my door, though." Then he asked, "Who's your friend?"

"You're Nash," Elle said.

"Answer me," Nash demanded as he ground the gun barrel further into her jaw.

"My name is Julian Saunders."

Nash leaned out slightly from behind Elle's head to get a clearer view. "I know you, don't I?"

"Ten years ago, Fallujah."

"That's it. The little self-righteous hajji lover."

"You murdered civilians," Julian said coldly.

"They're all animals. I did this world a favor. You just didn't have what it takes for war. Running off and crying to the brass like a little pussy."

"You were Johnathan West at the time. Nash was one of your aliases. You were supposed to be tried for war crimes. How are you here?"

"It's good to have friends with all the right connections. Ones that will be very happy to get their hands on this lovely piece of ass." Nash pulled her tight against him. Elle's mind raced, trying to figure out how to end the standoff. She needed Nash alive. It was the only way she'd get to Tom. But every scenario she thought of ended up with one of them dead.

If someone was going to die, she knew who had her vote.

"Port of Djibouti," Elle said. Julian's eyes locked on hers.

"What the fuck does that mean?" Nash barely got the last word out before Julian's bullet seared across her neck and tore through his eye.

The pressure against her body slid away. Elle's hand jerked to her neck, but she pulled it back from the flash of pain.

Julian was by her side in an instant. He kicked away Nash's gun, but that was just his training taking over. The brain matter on the wall behind them made it clear that Nash was dead. He cupped the opposite side of her head so he could look at the wound. "I wish you'd stop asking me to shoot you."

"At least this time, it's just a graze. Great shot." For just a moment, their eyes locked, and Elle felt…something. *Get your head in the game.* "We're not done yet. Get across the street and see if you can get the girl. I'll finish here."

The reminder about the girl across the street was all the nudge Julian needed to get back on task. "Watch your back. There are still too many unknowns in this building."

"Move fast. We have to assume someone in this neighborhood called in the gunshots. The real cops should be here any minute."

Elle stared down at Nash and felt frustrated. She had no choice. It was her, Julian, or Nash. She knew it, but what a loss. Still, there had to be something that could tell her how to get to Tom.

She started riffling through Nash's pockets when a bullet tore into the wall beside her. Elle rolled out of the way of the barrage that followed, narrowly escaping death. Staying low, she army crawled behind the sectional. The shooter was firing wildly from just inside the main door. *Amateur.* Elle popped up and returned fire at the first pause, striking a woman twice in the chest. She screamed and dropped the gun, falling back against the wall.

Leaping over the furniture, Elle ran to her and kicked the pistol out of the way. Then she checked the hallway to ensure there were no more re-enforcements coming her way. It was silent. In the heat of the moment, they passed the first apartment on this floor, which had the third woman helping the traffickers. She had to be the most loyal slave the traffickers had in their stable. Otherwise, they never would have allowed her to see freedom daily or arm her.

The woman was panting heavily and cursing. "You ruined everything, you fucking bitch."

She was a victim of the slave trade just as much as any of the others, but survival can take some dark turns. This woman wasn't part of her mission, and Elle didn't have time to waste.

Returning to the task at hand, she jogged down the narrow hallway where Nash had been lying in wait. There were two rooms, both doors were open. She quartered each opening as she approached to make sure they weren't occupied. One was full of brash décor, and the other was almost barren. Assuming that the barren room was for guests and not typically occupied, she started there.

A small, leather duffel was beside the bed. Elle threw it on top of the mattress as she continued to search the closet and dresser drawers. Empty. There was a cell phone and a watch on the nightstand. She threw them in the bag and left the room. Hopefully, something would prove useful.

The next room clearly belonged to the guard—there had to be a dozen selfies of him and some woman shoved into the frame of the wall mirror. Elle could feel the minutes flying by. Triaging the second bedroom, she selected the desk but found all the drawers locked. Out of time. This wasn't her primary objective, and she needed to stay on task.

Shouldering the leather bag, Elle walked back into the main room. The woman was struggling to breathe but alive. Snatching the phone out of the bag, she held it in front of Nash's face. It unlocked. Luckily, facial recognition software only required one good eye. *Who knew?* Breathing a sigh of relief that she might still be able to find the information she needed, Elle dialed 9-1-1 as she left the apartment.

"9-1-1, what's your emergency?"

"Send police and EMS. Now. Multiple gunshot victims, at least one is critical. There are also numerous sex-trafficking victims on site." Elle gave them the apartment address and the one for the townhome across the street as she walked out of the building. She hung up abruptly when she saw the door of the house with the teenage girl wide open and a body in the street.

Running toward the house, she paused at the body. It had to be one of the traffickers. He must have been coming to the apartment building as backup and encountered Julian instead. *Where is he?* Heart pounding, Elle ran to the house. Julian appeared just as she made the front stoop. The look on his face told her everything.

"They took her."

CHAPTER 7

Tuesday, 2330: Northern Virginia.

"We've got to go, Julian. Now."

They made their way behind the townhouse to the back alley that ran the length of the block. Keeping to the shadows as much as possible, they sprinted back toward the truck. Sirens were approaching. When they arrived at the end of the alley, Julian removed the police jacket, Elle let her hair down, and they put the badge and guns away. She handed him the duffel, and they stepped out onto the road holding hands. The slight adjustment to their appearance and change of demeanor should keep them from drawing the eye of the police. But it would only buy them a few seconds if anyone on the block was paying attention. Hopefully, that would be enough.

Red and blue lights started to reflect off every surface. They had cut the sirens, so the police cars had to be right on top of them. Nearing the truck, Elle moved to the driver's side just as the first cruiser rushed past them. This was followed in rapid succession by a second. As soon as they passed, Elle jumped behind the wheel and started the engine. Pulling away from the curb, she turned at the first intersection. She wanted to be out of sight as soon as possible.

"They'll have their hands full for a while, but it's not going to be long until they start questioning the neighbors. If anyone grabbed the plate number of this truck, they'll put out a BOLO within the hour," Julian said.

"It'll muddy the waters when the vehicle comes back to Officer Greg Bradley, the surname I told the neighbors. But the real Officer Bradley is a man who looks nothing like either of us. His service weapon was just to sell the role. I used my SIG, so none of the ballistics will trace back to him. Some suspicion might linger about him being a vigilante, but they won't be able to prove anything. It'll be circumstantial at best, and no DA is going to want to turn this case away for anything so easily disputed."

"So, what now?"

"I have a promise to keep, and then we need to disappear for the night. I need to tear that phone and bag apart. Without Nash, I've got nothing more to go on."

"We have the dirty cop's phone," Julian offered.

"And I should send you right back to HQ to get it exploited. But after losing two of his guys, Tom will be doubling down on his efforts to find me with whoever he has left. The surveillance on Tex did us a favor. Tom knows Tex couldn't have been with me tonight. He also knows how I operate—he expects me to go it alone if Tex isn't there. Having you with me adds another variable that Tom didn't account for. I need to take every advantage I can get."

"Happy to be of service."

"You say that now. How are you at stealing cars?"

"How about we just call a cab?" Julian asked.

"Are you kidding?"

"Do you want to blend in or not?"

"Okay. There's a gas station down the road from where we're going. I'll drop you off there with the bags. Use the gas station phone to call a cab. I'll do what I need to do and then hoof it back to you."

"Do I want to know?"

"Probably not."

"Just be careful. Please."

***

Elle returned to Officer Bradley's residence on heightened alert. Had he kept his word? Or was she walking into an ambush? She parked the truck in the designated spot, cleared the GPS, and got out as though she lived there. It was after midnight, and the apartment complex was quiet. She picked up her pace while keeping her senses attuned.

She made it to the apartment door without incident and edged it open. Bracing for an attack, opening the door felt like it took an eternity. Eventually, she could make out voices over the sounds of the TV playing in the background. It was Greg, swearing to his wife that he would make everything up to her. Elle stood in the doorway and listened for a few moments before stepping inside. Both Greg and his wife were bound and on the couch, as she'd left them. Such a personal conversation wasn't something they'd want to have within earshot of anyone if they could help it. This wasn't a setup.

"It may not seem like it now, but I did you both a huge favor tonight."

Her hostages jumped at the sound of her voice. And Carrie started to tremble.

"What do you mean?" Greg asked.

"Your partner brought new meaning to the term dirty cop. There will be an investigation, two of them, actually, and you will get questioned. A lot. Stick to the story I told you. You came home from work, and you and Carrie were here all night. No matter what they accuse you of, it won't stick. If you keep to the story."

"What do you mean? What will I be accused of?"

"Things you won't mind being accused of—but since they're illegal, I wouldn't advise taking credit." Elle placed his badge, unloaded service weapon, and keys on the kitchen counter and moved to stand in front of them. "You'll be getting a new partner. Chances are, a better one."

"Is Chris dead?" Greg asked.

"No. But he's going to wish he was. Chris is about to go through hell and then spend the rest of his life watching his back in prison."

"Did you set him up?"

"I exposed him for what he is."

"That's not an answer."

He's learning. "I set up the bust but not the crime. Everything they'll find is all Stokes. You need to distance yourself or risk getting pulled down with him. Follow my directions, and you'll both make it through this." Elle moved to Carrie. She stiffened.

"I'm going to release your hands, and then Greg's. Do not move until I'm gone. I'm still armed, and I don't want to have to kill you both after you've made it this far."

"Please. We won't do anything," Carrie said.

Elle uncuffed her and then turned her attention to Greg. "I'm trusting you to be smart, Greg. Don't make me regret it."

He lifted his cuffs. "It's not going to be a problem," he said, eyes on Carrie.

Watching him closely, Elle removed the cuffs and backed away. "Once I'm out the door, you can remove the cable ties around your ankles. Don't try to come after me."

"I won't," Greg said.

Elle believed him, but she still took off at a sprint once she closed the door, running hard all the way to the gas station, slowing once she came up to the side of the building. Shifting her stride to a fast walk, she rounded the corner. Julian was standing outside of a cab, leaning against the door.

"Was starting to think you got lost in the bathroom. You ready?" he asked audibly.

"More than ready. Sorry I kept you waiting," Elle said to the driver as she climbed in.

The driver pulled away a few seconds after the door closed. Elle shot Julian a look. *Where is he taking us?* Anxiety coursed through her veins, despite her best efforts to keep it at bay. It was making it almost impossible to keep her breathing even and her smile in place. What, really, did she know about Julian?

A warm hand covered hers and gripped it gently. Julian leaned in. "Trust me. You're going to love this place," he said.

Julian always seemed to see right through her and, yet, somehow remain a mystery. To say it was disconcerting was an understatement. Elle studied his face, looking for any sign of treachery. Nothing. Once again, her gut said he could be trusted. She nodded and tried to settle her nerves. Leaning into the seat, she focused on what she was feeling as Wise had instructed and let the feeling pass. Willing her heart rate to slow and her muscles to ease, her control returned.

The heat from Julian's body, so close to hers, pulled at her. His thumb was caressing the back of her fingers. Glancing his way, she saw that he was looking out the window, making the gesture seem absentminded. For some reason, that moved her. Despite having sex and then pushing him away, she still hadn't gotten Julian out of her system.

He mattered to her. And that was scary as all hell. Not to mention dangerous.

They headed south on Interstate 95, and, before long, they were taking an exit to Woodbridge, Virginia. They passed through a very commercial area into a residential one. The houses were older but in good repair. At the bottom of a hill, they crossed a bridge over a small waterway and turned into a neighborhood. The house they stopped at could have fit in anywhere. It was a modest, Cape Cod-style residence with a detached garage. The area felt a little claustrophobic, but the channeling they had just gone through would make it impossible for a surveillance team to enter undetected, and they were close enough to a major highway to disappear fast if need be.

Elle paid the driver with some of the cash she'd lifted from Stokes, and they got out of the cab. As they walked up to the house, she asked, "Is this your place?"

"No. It belongs to a friend. He's a security contractor. Just left yesterday for a year in the sandbox. I told him I'd keep an eye on it for him. Unless someone was listening in on my calls before all this started, nothing is connecting me to this place, so it should be as safe as any location to lay low."

"This should work. Good job."

There was a lockbox, similar to what realtors use when showing houses hanging on the door. Julian entered a code and took out the house key. Unlocking the door, he moved inside to disable the alarm. Flipping on a light switch, Elle took in her surroundings. It was the quintessential bachelor pad. Black, leather furniture, a giant TV, PlayStation, and an American flag coffee table that she was pretty sure had a hidden weapons drawer under the top.

"Do me a favor and check to make sure we're alone," Elle said.

Julian nodded and walked away without comment.

Elle took the duffel and set it on the coffee table. Sitting on the couch, she started to pull out all the contents: clothes, toiletries, wallet, phone, watch, Glock 27, three extra magazines, and a small bag of what appeared to be ecstasy. She riffled through the side pockets and then tore through the wallet for any information that could help her. Nothing. Except for two grand in cash.

Feeling desperation coming on, Elle snatched the cell phone and scrolled through Nash's calls and messages.

Julian returned. "We're good. The house is locked down. Everything is unplugged, and the fridge is empty. What's next?"

"Damnit!" Elle said as she threw the phone at an armchair.

"I take it Nash was better at operational security than your dirty cop."

"I've got nothing. Nash was the next rung on the ladder, and that's gone now."

"You don't know that yet. You still have both phones—maybe that's all Jack and Eve need."

Looking at the time, she knew there was nothing she could do tonight. It would have to wait until the morning, and then they'd have to get creative to get the phones to the team. She wanted to scream in frustration. The idea of having to delay any longer was making her crazy, but it couldn't be helped.

She needed to do something. Anything. "Is the water still working here?"

"I think so."

Elle grabbed her bag and headed toward the stairs to the second floor.

"I'll track down some food. But, we're going to be limited on options that deliver at this hour. How do you feel about pizza?" Julian asked.

Elle chuckled. "Why not? Anything but anchovies and peppers. Just use the cash in the duffel and give your friend's name. How are you going to make the order?"

"Landline is still working. The phone company either hasn't shut it off yet, or my buddy didn't bother to pause his service."

"Just make sure you can see both of the delivery person's hands when they give you the pizza."

"What?"

"Never mind. I'll be quick," Elle said as she walked up the stairs.

The second floor of the house was small, with two bedrooms and a full bathroom. Elle locked the bathroom door and got down to business. She didn't like feeling vulnerable, and she was feeling it now. Her instincts said that Julian could be trusted, but, for some reason, that didn't settle her nerves. She felt completely off balance with him, and she couldn't afford that.

Not now. Not ever.

Shower, food, new plan—then everything would be back on track. Peeling off her clothes, Elle frowned at the blood she found in her hair and on her clothes. No wonder the Bradley's reacted the way they had when they saw her. It was pure luck that it had been dark when they were getting into and out of the cab, and the driver hadn't been paying any attention to them. *Sloppy, Elle. Get it together.*

Rolling the clothes into a ball, Elle set them aside and took her toiletries into the shower. Her wounds were all weeping from the abuse she'd been putting them through. At this rate, she'd never heal all the way. She took a few extra moments to make sure she cleaned them thoroughly, and then she got the blood out of her hair. Getting out of the shower, she grabbed the first towel she saw. There was a slight odor to it. It had been used by the homeowner before he departed, but beggars can't be choosers.

She dried off and dressed, then repacked her gear. She wanted to be ready to move at a moment's notice. She pulled the trash bag from the can by the sink and shoved her dirty clothes in it. They didn't fit, but she didn't care. She just wanted to avoid getting blood and gunshot residue everywhere.

She returned to the living room. Julian was standing by the window watching the street.

"What's wrong?" she asked him.

"Nothing. Just couldn't relax. Figured I'd watch for the pizza guy. Should be here any minute."

Elle took her dirty clothes to the kitchen and put them in the bigger trash can. Then she grabbed a couple of glasses and some paper towels and returned to the living room.

"Thanks for your help tonight. Not sure how I would have pulled it off without the assist," Elle said.

"I don't buy that for a second. But you're welcome regardless."

"What can you tell me about Nash?"

"He was a contractor with one of the security firms that were making a killing in Iraq in the early days. My unit had been partnered with them a few times. There were rumors of some questionable activity, but nothing stuck. I hadn't dealt with them much and wrote off the stories as the fog of war. Never occurred to me they could be true."

"What happened?" Elle asked.

"We were doing some recon just outside of Fallujah when we heard gunshots. We took cover, but it was silent after that. I was about to make the call to get back on mission when Nash started shooting at an apartment building. The other contractors joined in, and a couple of my guys did too. I assumed he'd identified the threat and engaged. But I didn't see a threat when I looked through my scope. I saw civilians being gunned down. Women and children. No evidence of any weapons or hostile intent. I called for a ceasefire and demanded an explanation. Nash claimed he positively identified the shooter and that he had been taking out re-enforcements. I didn't buy it and went after Nash—hard. That's when the counterattack happened. We weren't paying attention, and two of my guys got hit. We ended up calling QRF to pull us out. I reported the incident as soon as we got back. The investigation took forever, but it led to Nash and one other guy being brought up on charges of war crimes. The others involved managed to convince the investigators they only fired because they believed they were being fired upon. The prosecutor didn't have enough to prove otherwise, so they got away with it. And I went to Captain's Mast for putting my guys in harm's way. If I hadn't picked a fight with Nash, the enemy wouldn't have been able to surprise us, and my guys wouldn't have been shot."

"Did they survive?"

"Fortunately, yes. But one will never walk again."

"What about the contractors?"

"Nash and his right-hand man were tossed in the detention facility after we got back and then transported out within a few days of the official charges being filed. It was a rough few days, though. The other contractors came after me a few times. Trying to get me to retract my statement. Didn't go so well for them, but I was still glad when it was over. Once Nash and his boy were gone, there was nothing they could do about it. Nash wasn't going to be allowed back in country regardless of the outcome of the investigation. It wouldn't have played out well for any of the leadership or the contracting company to bring him back. So the rest of the contractors didn't press things again. I always assumed Nash and his boy were rotting away in a hole somewhere."

"Who was the other man?"

"Don Krueger."

Elle returned to the kitchen and found a pad of paper and pencil left on the counter. Sitting back on the couch, she wrote down the name and stared at it. "It doesn't ring a bell, but it may be another lead for Jack and Eve to run down. What about the other guys involved? The ones that didn't get charged?"

"Jeff Hastings was the other contractor. Tim Boone and Seth Daniels were my guys."

Elle stopped writing when she heard the last name. "What do you know about Seth Daniels?"

"Not much. That was Seth's only tour, and he distanced himself from the incident as fast as he could. The wound he took wasn't serious, but he didn't stay in the teams long after that. He was using it as a steppingstone for his political run. He was more than capable but seemed more interested in padding his resume. He's a congressman now for Pennsylvania, I think."

"I need to get online, now."

"What's up?"

"I think you just handed me everything I need, but want to verify it."

"We can check the neighborhood for open Wi-Fi, but we'd have to use the stolen phones."

The doorbell rang, making them both jump. Elle moved to the side of the door and confirmed it was the pizza delivery kid. He looked like he had just turned eighteen. Smiling, Elle opened the door. "Awesome! You're just in time!"

The kid looked perplexed but returned her smile. "Uh, thanks?"

"You can help me win a bet. We're seeing who can go longer without using our devices, but now we have a debate to settle. Since we never said other people's devices were off-limits, I'll give you an extra twenty bucks if you'll let me google Congressman Seth Daniels on your phone. Or you can do it. His Wikipedia page should have everything I need to claim victory."

"Come on. That has to be cheating!" Julian said, playing along.

The kid mulled it over for a second but then shrugged. "Twenty bucks on top of a tip? Sure thing." He pulled out his phone and, after a few seconds of button mashing, handed it to Elle. "Is this what you need?"

Elle took the phone and scrolled through the Wiki page, scanning the contents. She froze halfway down when it talked about his family and their years of government service. One name leaped off the page. *Gotcha, you piece of shit.* She smiled victoriously, keeping up the façade. "I was right! He's got one sibling, a sister. Her name is Kimberly Daniels. Pay up, honey!"

Julian's face didn't betray that he recognized the name of Director Calloway's secretary, but Elle saw his muscles tense behind his smile. "You totally cheated. Can we at least eat now?"

Elle was just about to hand the phone back to the kid when a hyperlinked article caught her eye, and she felt her blood run cold. *No.* Clicking the link, a news article from two years ago popped up about a missing girl. Congressman Daniels' fourteen-year-old niece had disappeared without a trace. Despite all the Congressman's resources, they had no leads, and the case had gone cold. Elle clicked on the attached photo and turned it to Julian. His eyes narrowed as he struggled not to react.

It was the young girl from the trafficker's house. The one they hadn't been able to save.

CHAPTER 8

Wednesday, 0100: Woodbridge, Virginia

Tom has to be using the girl as leverage, right?" Julian asked.

"Against Calloway's secretary—maybe, but not the Congressman. Unless he was particularly close to the girl, chances are he's complicit. This is about getting access to the director's office."

"Close or not, she's family. How could anyone do that?"

"Do you need me to answer that?" Elle asked.

"No. I'll never understand it."

"And that's a good thing. It's one thing to know something like this exists; it's another to see it. Are you still with me?" Elle asked.

"Are you kidding?"

"Okay, then let's get to it. We need to get the team out of HQ without alerting Kim Daniels. Can't risk telling Calloway what we're doing—he'd never let this play out. How do you feel about adding a few more felonies to your resume?"

Julian laughed. "With the years we've earned already, I don't think it really matters. Might as well make it count."

Elle snagged a piece of pizza and kicked back on the couch. "We can't do anything until the morning, so let's eat and try and get some sleep. We need to be sharp tomorrow."

Julian joined her on the couch. "What's the plan?"

"We're going to get everyone out of the building and bring the team to us."

"Sounds good. How?"

"Still working on the details but, suffice it to say, it won't be subtle."

They sat in silence, eating pizza and drinking a couple of beers Julian had snagged from the fridge. Elle was just starting to relax when tension began to creep back in, and her appetite disappeared.

"What's wrong?" Julian asked.

How the hell does he always know? "Nothing."

"Are you ever going to trust me?"

"I trust you. You wouldn't be here if I didn't," Elle said, but Julian's expression made it clear he didn't believe her. She set down the half-eaten piece of pizza and met his eyes. "Look, if you haven't figured it out by now, I have a way of doing things. Alone. It's hard for me to adjust to having someone around, and I don't like distractions."

"I'm a distraction?" Julian asked as a smile tugged at the corners of his mouth.

Shaking her head, Elle tried to keep a straight face. "Barely know you're here."

He laughed. "And I thought you were a good liar."

"Is that a challenge?" Elle asked.

"Nope. But this is." Julian put down his drink and slid across the couch. He took the beer from her hands and leaned in close. "You're always pushing me away, but here I am, again. You don't want to let people in. I've been there."

Elle's body temperature kicked up along with her heart rate. "This is what I'm talking about. We need to stay focused." She started to move away. Julian's hand on her arm stopped her. She turned back and looked at him again.

Mistake.

She wasn't sure who moved first, but she was in Julian's arms, their faces inches apart. It took the full force of her will to stop herself from going farther. "What do you want from me?"

"You. For however long I can have you. But I'm hoping for more than one night this time."

"Why?"

"We connected the moment we met. That's never happened to me before. I understand you, even when we disagree. You matter to me. That makes this worth fighting for."

"I betrayed you."

"You betrayed yourself. We both know you were trying to run from anything that made you feel vulnerable. I knew it then, but my pride got in the way. Not this time. I'm calling you out. Tell me I'm wrong."

Elle's heart thundered in her chest so hard it hurt. The churn of emotions swirling around felt indistinguishable from each other—fear, desire, anxiety, longing—how was it possible to feel victorious and defeated simultaneously? She wanted to make everything stop but didn't know how.

Julian moved her hand to his chest. His heart was pounding, too.

The world stopped spinning, and she focused on him. "You're not wrong, but it's not that simple."

"Maybe not, but it doesn't have to be complicated either, Elle. What have you got to lose?"

"Myself."

"Only when you want to," Julian said as he leaned in and kissed her.

Elle didn't pull away again. Any thought of self-preservation disappeared as she lost herself in the moment. She'd never wanted a man the way she did this one. It terrified her, but her fear melted as the fire built between them.

***

Elle opened her eyes and, for a moment, forgot where she was. Her adrenaline spiked, and her muscles tensed just as an arm wrapped around her and pulled her close. The warmth and smell of Julian surrounded her. Somehow, they ended up in the master bedroom. The previous night had been an intense blur, not just physically but emotionally. In the heat of the moment, in the darkness, everything seemed possible.

Now, in the harsh light of day, Elle felt exposed.

"You're strong enough for this," Julian said.

Damnit. "Would you get out of my head?"

He kissed her gently, caressing her face. "Not a chance. That might be the only advantage I have."

Elle couldn't help but laugh. "Don't count on it." Her tension eased a bit. She couldn't deny that she liked it. Him. Julian fit in her world. But the emotions didn't.

"I can feel your wheels spinning, Elle. Talk to me."

"The path I'm on may end up being a one-way street. You need to know that. Whatever this is, shouldn't happen."

"Actually, I think it means it should. If you truly believe you're not going to win, then I'll ask you again—what have you got to lose?"

"I didn't say I wasn't going to win. But winning doesn't mean I walk away from this. Does that sound like an ideal time for a relationship?"

"There are no good times to start a relationship. You either take the chance, or you don't. Now stop stalling and answer my question."

"Kinda hate you right now," Elle said.

He smiled and kissed her. "I'll take that as you pleading the fifth."

Elle returned his kiss before pushing him away with a bit of reluctance. "We have work to do, Julian. Stop being a distraction."

"Yes, ma'am. What's our next move?'

"It's time for you to pay a visit to HQ."

"Just me?" he asked.

"Yes. I need you to get the team out and bring them here."

"What are you going to do?"

"Stir up some trouble."

CHAPTER 9

Wednesday, 0930: Washington, D.C.

Elle walked onto the platform at Union Station and pulled out her phone. Her hair was tucked up inside a ball cap, and she was wearing glasses to make it harder to ID her given that she now had a history with this place. She hadn't used the phone since she called Wise, but she had to assume it was on Tom's radar by now. But even if it wasn't, it was about to be. Elle powered it up and felt an inner "timer" start ticking. Dialing Director Calloway directly as she boarded her train, she hoped he would still take her call. If she could influence Calloway to look into Nash, that would send shockwaves through Tom's network. Elle wanted to divide all his resources, and then attack. The line rang several times before a woman's voice came on. Elle had planned for this possibility, but things would have been so much easier if Calloway had answered.

"Director Calloway's office," Kim Daniels said.

"Ms. Daniels. It's Elle Anderson. I need to speak with Director Calloway. It's important."

There was a long pause. Elle knew Daniels had to be clambering to alert people while figuring out how to answer her. Eventually, she said, "Ms. Anderson. Um, the director is very busy today. Was he expecting your call?"

"Is he ever?" Elle answered as the train started to pull out of the station. It would take a few minutes for whatever crew had been sent to intercept her to realize she was on a train. Once that happened, there would be a big scramble to redirect their assets, and the chase would be on.

"Would you like me to try and fit you into his schedule today?"

"You know me. I'm going to talk to him one way or the other."

"Let me see what I can do. Hold, please."

Smart move. Giving the illusion of searching for a timeslot would draw out the call. The longer the line stayed active, the easier it would be for Daniel's adversaries to track her down. This was a dangerous but necessary tactic. If Julian and her team had any hope of getting out of HQ without being followed, the distraction had to be one that Tom couldn't resist. But, if she played this out too long, there would be no escape, and Tom would win.

Elle waited a few minutes, then hung up and turned the phone off.

At the next stop on the train line, feeling a net closing in, Elle got out and flagged down a cab. If the timing was off on this at any point, they all would be done for. Sliding into the back of the cab, she did a quick assessment of the driver. So far, so good.

A black sedan shot past them and stopped by the train platform as they pulled away from the curb. Two men in dark suits got out and rushed the train. She was inside the net now. That couldn't have been the only team sent after her. Where were the others? Just then, a glint of light caught her attention, and she ducked down reflexively. Glass shattered all around her, and the cab driver started freaking out.

There's no way they got a positive ID that fast. Either Tom was desperate and no longer cared about exposing his network, or more wannabe assassins looking for a payday had been hired. Elle guessed the second. "Turn and get us out of here!" Elle shouted at the driver.

The man was panicking in at least two different languages, but he kept the car on the road. Mostly. Peering over the seat, Elle chanced a look around. She needed to try and find the shooters if there was any chance of getting out of this. She didn't have to look hard.

A silver Mercedes was gaining on them, fast. It must have turned when they did and were now in pursuit. There was no way the cab could outrun it. They had to either lose it or fight…or maybe they could have someone else fight for them.

"Drive to the nearest police station!" Elle ordered. Then she did the last thing anyone expected her to do—she turned on the phone and dialed 9-1-1.

"Please, help us. Someone is chasing us on the highway. He's got a gun, and he's trying to kill us!" Elle called out the mile markers, identified the cab, and avoided answering any personal questions by portraying a woman on the verge of a panic attack.

"Help is on the way, ma'am, just stay on the line," the dispatcher said.

Elle barely heard the woman. She was too busy watching the Mercedes line up for a pit maneuver. "Hit the brakes. Now!" she ordered. She wasn't sure the driver would listen, but he did. He slammed on the brakes so hard, for a second, Elle thought the car was going to flip. But, instead, the Mercedes flew by, as anticipated, and was a couple of hundred feet up by the time they slowed down enough to turn and double back.

"Go, now! Turn off here," Elle shouted.

The cab driver stomped on the gas pedal. The tires squealed before they gripped the road and propelled them forward. The Mercedes was driving against traffic to make its way back to the exit, buying them space. Leaving the highway meant more hazards in the roadway. *Definitely not the prime place for a high-speed chase.* But it was perfect for an escape. Seeing a grocery store to their right, Elle ordered the driver to turn in. He seemed hesitant until she told him they could ditch the car fast and hide inside. His hesitation disappeared.

They whipped through the parking lot of Giant Food, causing people to either protest or grab their damn phones. Elle pulled the hat down lower, preparing to hit the pavement at a run when the taxi stopped. Checking behind them, she saw the silver Mercedes gaining ground. Elle relayed their location to the 9-1-1 dispatcher and hung up the phone.

"We need to get to the doors so we can get inside before they start shooting at us again." The driver didn't respond, but his white-knuckle grip on the steering wheel navigated well and did the talking for him. Hand on the door handle, Elle waited for the vehicle to slow. *Déjà vu.* At least this time, she wouldn't be injured, like when she jumped from the ambulance in Rome.

The cab screeched to a halt at the front of the store. Elle was out the door and on the run. And, surprisingly, the driver was right behind her.

"Active Shooter! Get inside! Lock the doors!" Elle screamed as she ran through the entrance. She kept spreading the word as she ran through the store. People almost immediately stopped paying attention to the crazy woman running through the store as panic took hold about the threat in the parking lot. Using the chaos as a shield, the cab driver lost in the fray, Elle tossed the phone and ran to the storage area in the back, looking for the rear exit.

Any minute, the shooters, or the cops, would come in looking for her. The police were just a means to an end. In this case, taking care of her latest assailants. The shooters from the Mercedes would have to break off chasing her to either escape or fight with the cops.

Seeing an exit, she hit it at full stride. In the back of the store was a small parking area, and, other than some dumpsters, it was wide open. She crossed the distance at a dead sprint and kept right on going. She needed to put as much space between her and the scene as possible. She ran through several other parking lots before slowing down and taking stock of the situation.

The business district was giving way to an area that was predominately hotels. Perfect. Pulling off her hat and jacket, she walked toward the highest amount of foot traffic with the intent of blending in. Selecting the Hilton, Elle pulled out her Sarah Smith ID and some cash. No credit card this time. It may have been a long shot, but she couldn't risk that Tom's people had found her last hotel stay. The name would be vague enough to use again, but the credit card number would jump out.

Approaching the counter, she asked the receptionist, "I just got a fraud alert for my card. Is it okay for me to use cash until I figure out what's going on?"

"That's terrible. I'm so sorry. Uh, yeah, we can do that for now. Once you have everything sorted out, just bring the card back to us, and we can switch over the payment type. Do you have a reservation?"

"No, I was going to stay across the street, but the girl behind the counter couldn't figure out how to check me in without a credit card. I was hoping I'd have better luck here."

"Happy to help. We have rooms available, so it's no problem. Can I see your ID?"

Elle handed him the driver's license. Moments later, she was on the elevator, room key in hand, heading to the fourth floor. As soon as she was in the room, Elle engaged the security lock and went to the window. The angle wasn't perfect, but she could see enough to know that the police had arrived at the Giant Food in full force. She could just make out a roadblock and the flash of red and blue lights.

Checking the time, she estimated it would be at least another hour before her team made it back to the safehouse. With the police so close, the best thing she could do now was lay low and wait for the right time to move again. At least the police presence should discourage any more assassination attempts. But the police were only half her problem. Using cash to get the room could draw attention from Tom's people. Once Tom found out she'd escaped from his latest batch of hired guns, the search would be on. He'd be looking for anything that could point to her. Cash payment at a hotel would make that cut.

She hadn't made it out of the net yet.

She spotted the hotel information binder on the desk. Looking at the map inside, she identified a bus stop two blocks away and a train station about half a mile past that. *Bus it is.* Hitting the bathroom, she washed her face and then braided her hair. Tying the jacket around her waist, she tucked the ball cap into the small of her back. She wanted to be ready to move at any time. Returning to the window, she sat in the chair and watched the activity on the road. If the police got the shooter from the Mercedes, the cordon wouldn't push out past the area around the crime scene. But if anyone else escaped, the police would expand into a grid search, and the perimeter would be extended for miles. They'd be looking for her. For now, the cops would have their hands full with witnesses at the scene.

If she moved too soon, she risked being spotted in the initial canvass. Too long, and it would allow Tom's people to home in on her. Flipping on the TV, Elle selected a local news channel. Nothing yet. If she still had a phone, she'd check social media to see what was going on. Hard money said someone recorded everything and posted it somewhere, maybe even streamed it live. But, for now, she'd have to go off what she could see out the window and trust her gut.

Time crept by. More cop cars arrived, and then a helo. It took about fifteen minutes before Elle saw news trucks getting stopped at the police barricade. Flipping the channel to match the news van on the scene, Elle listened to the initial reports. There was a standoff inside the grocery store. At least two shooters got trapped inside when the police arrived. There were dozens of hostages. *Shit.* This was going to take a while, and the police presence was going to get heavier. News crews and onlookers, too.

The bright side was this meant crowds to blend into. The downside—it would be a significant amount of exposure. The chance of someone identifying her would be high. Not to mention it would make it harder to spot threats until they were right on top of her.

Nothing quite like the feeling of being a wanted fugitive in the middle of a crisis situation.

Fuck it. Time to move. Turning off the TV, Elle used the peephole to check the hallway before opening the door. She couldn't see any movement, so out she went, returning to the elevator. She would have preferred the stairs but going down four flights was not something most people staying in a hotel like this would do. Keeping up appearances would keep her under the radar.

Elle felt her tension kick up a notch the moment the elevator doors closed. What would she see when the doors opened? She watched the floor numbers descend and fought to keep up her façade. The camera over her left shoulder was capturing her every move. Who was watching her right now?

When the doors opened, Elle realized she had been holding her breath. Letting it out slowly, she smiled at the man at the reception desk and walked out of the lobby. Putting her sunglasses on, Elle walked to the bus stop, matching the flow of foot traffic around her. There wasn't as much as before, but enough that her presence wasn't an oddity.

Several people already waiting at the bus stop gave her a plausible reason to stand behind the glass alcove, which provided more screening from view. As they waited, one squad car passed by but didn't slow. More support? Elle didn't like it. She was just about to move on to the train station when the bus arrived.

Here we go.

CHAPTER 10

Wednesday, 1300: Woodbridge, Virginia

Two hours later, Elle walked into the safehouse. She barely stepped inside the door before she was assaulted. The fierce hug was nothing compared to the barrage of questions her analyst, Eve James, hurled at her. Elle struggled to identify individual words.

"Help, please," Elle said as Tex walked up. But, instead of rescuing her, he wrapped his arms around both of them.

"Guys, I can't breathe!"

"Breathing is overrated," her tech expert, Jack Paulson, said as he joined the group hug.

Elle looked over Eve's shoulder and saw Julian leaning against the back of the couch.

"Are you going to give me a hand?"

"Sure." Julian started clapping.

"Thanks, smartass. Okay, guys, I missed you, too. But we've got work to do."

"You're not getting off the hook that easily, Elle. You promise not to hold out on us?" Tex asked. "No matter what? Do we have a deal?" He hugged her a little tighter.

"This is extortion," Elle said.

"Yes or no, Elle?"

"Fine, yes." They released her. It had been just over a week since she had last seen her team, but considering the circumstances, it felt like forever. Burned by Tom, her career was over, and she was facing the very real possibility of being brought up on criminal charges. She had been spiraling deeper and deeper into a dark place. Elle had wanted to distance herself from them as much as possible to keep from taking them down. They were the only people in the whole world who mattered to her.

"Okay, I'll bring you up to speed. Julian, can you turn on the news?"

"Which channel?"

"Any of them," Elle said.

Julian flipped on the news, and they saw the coverage of the standoff at the Giant Food. It looked like the shooters were in custody now. They watched the report in silence for a few minutes before Julian said, "I know you said you were going to create some trouble, but don't you think this is a little over the top?"

"I had some party crashers that upped the game quite a bit. Tom is getting reckless. Which is going to make him more dangerous. You need to understand the stakes here."

After listening to the reporter for a few minutes, Eve asked, "They shot at you in front of civilians?"

"They would have shot into a crowd on the off chance

of wounding me. These guys were blunt instruments, not scalpels. If I had to guess, Tom put a bounty on me. Which means every lowlife in the area will be looking to cash in and make a name for themselves. Add in that we've still got Tom and his network of spies and mercenaries to deal with—that I'm on every law enforcement agency's most wanted list—and we are trapped between a rock and a hard place."

Turning off the TV, Elle faced her team, making sure they saw how serious she was. "Tom wants me dead at any cost. It's personal for him, has been since he was my handler. But now, his network has just as much to lose. They're going to fight to keep from being exposed. And by having his insiders label me a criminal, Tom's made it so that even the good guys are a threat. Everything I'm about to do is off the books. There is no top cover, no authorization. It's all highly illegal. The only reason you're here right now is because I need your help. If I can get to Tom, I can end this. But, given the circumstances, I won't blame you if you want out. I'll even help you find a place to hide until this is over."

"I'm in. I did have a massage and pedicure planned for this afternoon, but I can reschedule," Tex said.

"You said you need our help. That's all I needed to hear. I'm staying with you," Eve said.

"I couldn't bring all my gear with me, but I've borrowed the neighbor's Wi-Fi, and I've started tearing into the phones Julian gave me. If there's anything there, I'll find it," Jack said.

"Julian, thank you for everything you've done. It's not

too late to back out. I've already dragged you far enough down the rabbit hole."

"Not a chance, Elle. I'm with you, every step of the way," Julian said.

"Famous last words. Okay, let's do this," Elle said.

She gathered them in the living room and started with the ambush at her residence. She didn't leave out any details, which caused quite a stir more than once. Their reactions would have been comical under any other circumstances. No one interrupted her, but Elle stopped after telling them they found the Congressman's missing niece and about the connection to Tom when she saw Eve's face. A mix of horror and denial marred her features, and her whole body tensed.

"What is it, Eve?" Elle asked.

"I have a horrible feeling I know what's going on, Elle. But it's too awful to even think about, and I'm afraid to say anything in case I'm wrong."

"I trust your assessments. But if it helps, just tell me what you know—just the facts. And we'll go from there."

"Yesterday, I noticed some photos when I was walking by Calloway's office on Kim Daniels' desk. They were of a young girl. When I asked her about them, she told me they were her daughter, Anne. Anne has been missing for two years. Apparently, she was a troubled girl. Kim was a single mother and struggled with trying to handle Anne on her own, so her parents stepped in to help. Before she went missing, Anne came back to stay with Kim because her grandparents couldn't handle her anymore. But things didn't go well."

"Let me guess, Anne ran away," Tex said.

Eve nodded. "That's what Kim says. Just after her brother got her into some pricey boarding school."

"But you don't believe her. Why?" Elle asked.

"At the time, I thought it was just a coping mechanism. But now, I'm not so sure. The way she talked about her daughter sounded rehearsed. It wasn't so much what she was saying, but how she said it. And she spent more time talking about all the charities she supports in her daughter's name and how focusing on her career got her through the tough times."

Elle felt ill. "I see where you're going with this."

"I don't. What are you guys talking about?" Jack asked.

"Either Kim Daniels, or her brother, sold her daughter to the traffickers."

Silence met Elle's blunt response.

"No way. There's no way a family does that. Right?" Jack asked, not wanting an answer.

"One way or the other, Kim Daniels knows more than she's letting on. I think she found herself dealing with an out-of-control teenager and asked for help. Whether she knew what would happen at the time is tough to say. There's a possibility she doesn't know about the trafficking, but she's got to know about her brother's involvement in the disappearance. Somehow, they've used that to leverage her into becoming a mole inside the Director's office. The reason the story sounded rehearsed when Kim talked about Anne is because it was. It's the cover story they made her memorize."

"Shit. It was a setup. Kim provides Tom access to everything at the CIA, or she gets framed for selling Anne," Tex said.

"Please, tell me we're wrong," Eve pleaded.

"I wish I could, Eve. You knew it the second we connected the Congressman to Tom, didn't you?"

"When you said you found Anne, I was excited because I thought with proof of life, the case would be reopened," Eve said. "Kim told me there are too many missing kids for them to keep at it without any leads. I felt bad for thinking it, but I'd wondered why the Congressman hadn't intervened. Now, I think we know."

"I don't buy it. We've got to be missing something here. I was raised by a single mom—there's no fucking way," Julian said.

"You may be right, but we can't rule it out. Don't let your personal bias cloud your judgment. They're not all like your mom," Elle said.

"Like 'my' mom? What about yours?"

"She died when I was ten. And while they didn't sell me, I was nothing but a payday to the so-called moms I ended up with."

The silence that followed her blunt declaration made Elle realize how much she'd just given away. *What the fuck…?* Eve looked like she was about to say something conciliatory and moved to embrace her. Elle held up a hand. She didn't want to be touched right now.

"We'll spare you the details, Julian, but this isn't our first rodeo when it comes to dealing with the trafficking world. Three years ago, Elle and I found a smuggling route being used by covert agents from some of our biggest "fan clubs" to get in and out of the U.S. Thing is, when your business is moving people around under the radar, chances are not all of the "cargo" is there of their own free will. We got up close and personal with a lot of the scum who treat humans like cattle—and their victims. Bottom line, you don't want to know how often families sell their kids," Tex said.

"But it is possible Kim Daniels had no idea what was happening until it was too late, right, Elle?" Eve seemed to want that reassurance. For all of them.

Elle shrugged but nodded.

"She could be just trying to keep them both alive," Tex said.

"So, what do we do now?" Julian asked.

"We're going to have to draw the Congressman out. I'm not interested in going toe-to-toe with the Secret Service...right now, at least. And severing Tom's access to CIA operations is a priority, so Kim Daniels is our next target. Jack, we need to make sure no one can track us here if we set off a virtual tripwire. Whatever you need to do to make sure we stay off the grid, do it. Then I need you to tear those phones apart. Find me anything they've tried to hide, any possible connections to Tom or other members of his network. Eve, deep dive on both Kim Daniels and the Congressman. I want everything you can dig up—starting with where they live. Then build me a pattern of life."

"What about Mahmud Hussein, target Number 3? Where is he in all this?" Eve asked.

"He's another pawn in Tom's game. When I mentioned Number 3 to Tom earlier, he didn't react. No taunting, just basic allusions to a master plan. He used Number 3 to get in my head, hoping it would split my focus, but he's too much of a fanatic to keep in play. Tom's cashing in a lot of chips coming after me now. There's no way he's going to risk it blowing up in his face by bringing a known terrorist into the states with a vendetta of his own. Number 3 is probably tucked away somewhere, licking his wounds while he waits for his next shot at the title. I'll deal with him once his benefactor is out of the picture," Elle said.

"Shouldn't we be bringing Calloway in?" Tex asked.

"He'd never sanction any of this. And there's no way to alert him without potentially alerting Tom, too."

"What about Wise?" Julian asked.

"Tom's people have to be watching him like a hawk right now. I don't want to contact Wise again unless we have no choice."

"Pretty sure Wise thought of that," Tex said as he handed her a folded-up piece of paper. "He asked me to give this to you. Looks like an electronic dead drop."

Elle opened the page and saw a generic email address and a random alphanumeric password. Both her and Wise would be able to log onto the same email and use draft messages to communicate. Since they never actually got sent anywhere, there wasn't a trail unless you knew where to look. It was an old trick but could still be useful if they were careful. Elle memorized the information and then destroyed the piece of paper.

"So, what do we do while the wonder twins do their thing?" Tex asked.

"We're going to plan an ambush, but we have some prep work to do first," Elle said. She walked into the dining area, pulled the duffel bags they'd taken the night before out of a closet, and placed them on the table. Then, sliding the larger bag over to Tex, she said, "We didn't have a chance to check these out yet. Let's see what we have to work with."

Tex opened the bag and squealed like a happy kid. "Is that a Benelli M4 shotgun? Wonder if I can customize it like they did for John Wick?"

"Focus, fanboy. We need function checks and ammo counts on everything."

"Yes, Mom."

The smaller bag she'd taken from Nash had a Glock 29 and several magazines. She passed them to Julian. But otherwise, it was a bust, just clothes, toiletries, a pocketknife, and a Rolex watch. Elle examined every piece and the bag itself to make sure that she didn't miss anything. While the gun and ammo would come in handy, the phone seemed to be the only thing of value. Hopefully, Jack will be able to find something on it.

Looking across the table, she saw two AR-15s, the shotgun, and five pistols, but not much in the way of ammunition. Damn. "How are we looking?"

"The guns are in great shape. Their last owner may be a piece of shit, but the guy took care of his weapons," Julian said.

"We've got a couple of extra magazines for everything here, but I don't think we have enough rounds to fill them," Tex added.

"Go ahead and start jamming all the mags to see where we end up. I'm going to check on what the kids have so far," Elle said.

"It's only been ten minutes. Jack and Eve are the best, but you gave them one hell of a task," Tex said.

"I'm not looking for a finished product, just a place to start. In a war like this, whoever strikes first has the advantage.

We can't let that be Tom again."

Eve and Jack were in the living room, absorbed in their work. "Got anything?" Elle asked.

Jack didn't even look up. "Started with the phone call log, which hadn't been deleted. Pretty sure you said it was the one that belonged to the cop. I'm working on eliminating any number that is connected to his job. There may be other dirty cops but, without any text or audio, I'm not going to be able to tell what's legit and what might not be."

"Use the number for the other phone to narrow the field even further. Then, check for any calls or texts that came in before or after each time that number pops up," Elle directed.

"Good call. I'm on it," Jack said.

"What about you, Eve?"

"I have Kim Daniels' address and a listed number. Guessing it's a landline. I'm combing through her social media now to piece together her typical schedule," Eve said.

"Can you show me her house?"

"It looks like she has a condo in a gated community in Tyson's Corner," Eve said as she turned the laptop screen toward Elle. Studying the screen, she didn't like what she saw. The location was the last place anyone would choose for an ambush. It would be hard enough to get her team in, let alone get them out with their target. "Jack, do you have a tablet we could use to plan with?"

"Yeah, Eve and I both have tablets and our laptops. I wanted to bring more, but Julian said we had to move fast. The Cellebrite that I'm using to rip the phones you gave me was on a desk on our way out, so I, uh, borrowed it."

"Good thinking. Can I get one of those tablets?"

"Here you go," Eve said. She handed Elle an iPad.

Both were so intent on their tasks that they seemed to forget she was there. Elle left them to it.

Pulling up the location on the iPad, she set it down on the table. "Here's where our target lives. To call it less than ideal would be a slight understatement."

"We could go in the early morning, before dawn. Even good security can lose its edge during the time just before first light," Julian said.

Nodding, Tex said, "Jack can dismantle their cameras and the electronic access points. We may be able to just walk in without anyone being the wiser."

"If we were going to kill our target, that would be the way to go. But we need her alive, and trying to sneak back out with a captive might prove problematic. But you just gave me an idea." Elle looked at the surrounding area from the target location and smiled. "It's a heavily populated area. Lots of businesses and residences, but there are only two ways in or out of the complex. Both go to the main road. Going in would take balls or desperation—and I'm betting Tom thinks I have both. Let's use that."

"I'm confused. Are we going in or not?" Tex asked.

"We're going to make them think we are."

"How?" Julian asked.

"We'll get Jack to knock her security system offline and spoof Kim's landline number. I'll call and provoke her, from what looks like her home phone, then we'll trip the alarm. Kim will have to leave HQ and head home to deal with the responding officers and determine what I may have done.

That's when we grab her—while she's in transit."

"With everything going on, they're going to have someone keeping tabs on her. Maybe even a whole surveillance team or protective detail," Julian said.

"You're right, but what do you think their priorities are? Watch her? Or me?"

"Please tell me you're not going to make yourself bait again."

"Only if I have no other choice. I'm hoping to be able to ID any mobile surveillance before we make our move. If they're using static surveillance, then we need to be in and out before they realize what's happening and call in re-enforcements."

"We don't have the manpower for any counter-surveillance, let alone an ambush in a highly-populated area. How the hell are we going to do this?" Tex asked.

"Jack," Elle said.

"Not following. I know Mr. Wizard can do things that I can't spell, but I don't think he has cloning powers yet. Does he?" Tex asked, feigning concern.

Chuckling, Elle said, "Don't worry, the world can only handle one Jack. And that's all we need right now. That and two vehicles."

"You're going to box her in? What about the surveillance team?" Julian asked.

"Want to take a guess what his answer will be when I ask him if he can get us access to all the traffic cameras between HQ and our ambush site."

Tex snorted. "He'll be offended we even asked. That's child's play." Then, he added, "That's brilliant. Using the traffic cameras as our own static surveillance network. We should be able to ID any tails within a few turns. What about the vehicles?"

"A couple of grand and some private auto sales should get us what we need. I saw a printer upstairs and have no doubt that Jack can forge some temp tags for them."

"Won't that be strange? Aren't you worried about the seller thinking something illegal is going on?" Julian asked.

"Cash in hand usually ends any discussion. But if that doesn't ease their minds, then hearing that the vehicles are going to be demolition derby cars should explain why the tags are temporary," Elle said.

"That's just crazy enough; it may work."

"Crazy is what I specialize in. Tex, you're the car guy. Go snag Jack's tablet and find us some cars for sale by the owners. We're going to want things that run and can withstand fender-benders."

"On it," Tex said.

"Julian, you and I are going to map out the most likely routes and determine the ambush site and decision points."

"How long do you think we'll need to see if the target is being followed?"

"Depends on the size of the team. The more vehicles involved, the harder it will be. We need to give ourselves as many direction changes as we can."

"Then we have a problem. There aren't many changes, and it's mainly well-traveled roads."

Taking a hard look at the map, Elle studied the route, pulling up the satellite images to get a better feel for the area. "Then we grab her the second she gets off Dolly Madison Blvd. A vehicle ahead and a vehicle behind to force her to stop. We'll have to be fast and aggressive. If there's a tail, we need to be ready for a gunfight."

"In broad daylight?"

"Yep. Our target and any security will be on edge, but they'll be even more vigilant at night. We need to use whatever angles we can to succeed."

"Say this works, then what? What do we do with her? Julian asked.

"We're going to need someplace off the grid, not here. Isolated. Any thoughts?

"Maybe. How do you feel about a road trip?"

CHAPTER 11

Thursday, 1000: McLean, Virginia

"Ready, Jack?" Elle asked.

His disembodied voice came through the speakerphone on the dash of the old truck Elle was sitting in a mile west of the CIA Headquarters, in Langley. "Tell me when."

"Let's do it," Elle said.

"Okay. Go."

Elle dialed Kim Daniels' desk number on another pay-as-you-go phone and waited. If the woman wasn't sitting there, the plan would need some serious modifications.

The line clicked on, followed by a timid, "Hello?"

"Now, Kim, as Director Calloway's secretary, don't you have a more professional greeting?"

"Are you…in my house?"

"Don't worry, I didn't do any damage. Nice place."

"What do you want?"

"To talk. You and me. Face-to-face."

"Why?"

"You know why."

"I'm going to call the police."

"Pretty sure your alarm company did that for you. Doesn't matter, I won't be anywhere near your house when they arrive. Although, you may want to be. The cops will want you to walk through with them to see if anything is missing. There won't be. But there will be a gift. Just for you. And your brother."

"What are you talking about?"

"I'm talking about your daughter, Kim. I know what happened to her. Figured you might like a little proof-of-life. Wonder what the cops will think if they find it first?"

Silence.

Elle glanced at her watch. "Well, it's time for me to go. We'll chat soon." Hanging up, she looked over at Julian, behind the wheel of the beat-up F-150 they were sitting in. "We're on."

"So, I take it Jack was able to convince her that you were calling from inside her house?"

"I heard that. Of course, it worked. And Kim's alarm company called in a possible break-in. The cops should be on their way."

"Never doubted you for a moment, Jack," Elle said. "Now, I need you and Eve to be our eyes and ears. Tell us when you see her leaving. It should be soon. Tex, are you in position?"

"Yes, ma'am. Just hanging out at Starbucks, waiting for the green light."

"Once we get rolling, we'll be there in about fifteen minutes unless traffic takes a turn," Elle said.

"Copy all."

Elle sat back in the seat and tried to relax. They'd spent the previous evening planning for this moment. They were as ready as they were going to be. Feeling eyes, she looked over to see Julian watching her. Her body warmed on its own accord. She'd spent the last two nights wrapped in his arms and, while it had been worth it at the time, now she wasn't so sure. Distractions could be lethal in situations like this.

"What?"

He leaned forward and hit the mute button on the phone on the dash. "This life suits you."

"What makes you say that?"

"Everything about you seems more alive when you're working. I can see why you're as good as you are."

"But?"

"What are you going to do when this is over? Even after you get clear of this, the damage Tom did will still be there. I can't see the Agency ever letting you back in the field, and you'd never settle for a desk job."

"I can't let myself think about that right now. One problem at a time."

"Fair enough." Switching topics, Julian turned off the mute button and asked, "Are we taking bets on the size of her protective detail?"

"Can't we just stay positive and say that there won't be any?" Eve's worried voice chimed in over the conference call.

"Best we can hope for is just one vehicle. They'd want to keep watch on Kim, but since she's at HQ every day, they can't send a team in without drawing attention. They would be set up in a public area outside the security zone of the facilities and be ready to jump in behind her the moment she passes by," Elle said.

"Might be double that now, with all the hits Tom's network has been taking lately," Tex added.

"Heads up. Kim is on the move. Traffic camera has her approaching the on-ramp to Dolley Madison westbound," Jack reported.

"Jack, I need you and Eve watching her on any cameras you can access. Call out the first five cars behind her, and then keep an eye on them." As she was talking, Julian put the truck in gear. Two quick right turns, and they were on Dolley Madison, moving with traffic flow half a mile ahead of their target.

"We see two vehicles behind her, Elle. A silver pickup and a black sedan."

"Thanks, Eve. Julian, Tex, I have eyes on. She's three cars back and gaining."

Julian increased his speed to stay ahead of the speeding car. "I see her. She's obviously in a hurry. Guess you hit all the right notes with that phone call."

"Don't increase speed too much. We don't want to look like we're trying to stay ahead of her. Tex, if she ends up passing us, you'll need to take the front position. One way or the other, be ready to go in about six minutes."

"Ready here. Even got my macchiato to-go, just in case," Tex said.

"Diva."

"A man has needs, Elle."

Smiling, Elle returned her attention to the rearview mirror. The sleek, blue BMW was one car behind them now, and she seemed to be edging up to pass. This was going to be close. "I can see a silver truck and black sedan behind her still. We need to assume these are more hired guns. If they make the turn, taking them out is crucial."

"She's behind us now. If she keeps this pace, then she's going to pass us before the turn," Julian said.

"If she does, let her. Just don't let any other vehicle get between us once she does."

The BMW picked up speed until it was tailgating them, even though Julian was driving ten miles over the speed limit. Then, finally, Kim pulled out and sped past them, with their exit in sight. "You're lead now, Tex. Go!" Elle said.

"Moving."

Elle watched an old Chevy Impala pull out from a shopping complex as they exited onto Old Courthouse Road. It cut off the BMW causing the driver to brake hard to avoid a wreck. The median kept the BMW from going around the Impala, but Kim's impatience was evident as she was tailgating the other car. Both the truck and the sedan were trapped behind their F-150. As the Impala and the BMW crossed Wall Street, Elle said, "Now, Tex."

The Impala's brake lights came on suddenly, and tires barked in protest. The BMW didn't stand a chance. Brake lights flashed as Kim slammed on her brakes, but she still hit the older car.

Julian braked hard, halting all the vehicles behind them.

Elle jumped out and ran to the driver's side window of the BMW. Using the glass breaker tip on her knife, she smashed it and opened the door. The airbag had deployed, and Kim Daniels was disoriented. Reaching across the woman to undo the seat belt, she snatched her cell phone from the center console. Then, pressing the muzzle of her pistol into Kim's temple, Elle said, "No sudden movements. Your survival depends on your cooperation. Get out of the car, now."

The engine of the old pickup truck roared to life as Julian gunned it, driving in reverse. Elle had a split second to register the man with the machine gun before he jumped out of the way and then the crash of metal on metal. As soon as he stopped, Julian was out of the cab and running toward them. Gun in hand as he watched for the threat to regroup. Grabbing Kim by the hair, Elle ripped her from the BMW. She screamed but moved. Elle arrived at the Impala, shoving Kim along, gun in her back, just as Tex got out and started firing behind them. "Move, move, move!" he said.

Tearing the rear door open, she pushed Kim inside and slid into the back seat with her. Seconds later, Julian jumped in the passenger seat and Tex in the driver's seat. They peeled out and went speeding away toward the main drag. Time to disappear.

"Talk to me, Jack," Tex said into another cell phone on the dash of the Impala.

"9-1-1 calls just hit dispatch. You've got units on patrol to the east and west of you. Best guess, you've got five minutes."

Tex turned north on Leesburg Pike and kept pace with the other cars. As soon as they passed under Dulles Access

Road, he turned left into the first neighborhood. They moved through the residential streets until they came to a wooded area next to a tennis court. Parking next to an old, white Honda Civic with cheap baby sunscreens covering the rear windows, Tex cut the engine. He got out to look around before signaling for Elle to bring out their prisoner.

"Don't try anything, Kim. It wouldn't go well for you."

She nodded. Julian opened the door for them and held onto Kim as Elle got out. He had blood running down the side of his face.

Leading Kim to the Civic, Elle asked, "You okay?"

"Just a scratch. I'll be fine," he said.

"I broke a nail covering you guys, anyone going to ask how I'm doing? Or say thank you?" Tex asked.

"Suck it up, princess." Grabbing the phone in Julian's hand, Elle asked, "Jack, any roadblocks in our path?"

"They've cordoned off the ambush site and called in for backup. That place is going to be crawling with every cop in the area soon. I would get moving."

They piled into the Civic and continued north until the road turned east and brought them back to Leesburg Pike. Then, they turned south to use the Dulles Access Road to get to 495 South.

For the first ten minutes, they rode in silence. "Alright, we're on the highway heading to our next location. Jack, Eve, pack it up and get moving. Keep monitoring the police comms while you're on the move. Let us know if anything changes."

"See you soon, Elle," Eve said before the line disconnected.

Elle leaned back in the seat and studied her target. Kim

Daniels was wearing an expensive tailored suit, her hair and makeup were in disarray, and she had a few contact burns from the airbag. The woman's jewelry was expensive, as were her shoes. She clearly enjoyed splurging on herself.

"So, how did it all start, Kim? Was it the money or helping you get rid of your daughter that put you in Thomas Matthews' pocket?"

"My daughter ran away. She was troubled."

"Troubled or not, she didn't deserve to be sold as a slave."

"I don't know what you're talking about."

"Interesting response. You didn't even flinch at hearing the word slave. You already know where she is, don't you?"

"How dare you!"

"I saw your daughter—Anne—last night. She looked healthy, but we both know that looks can be deceiving. The men holding her had to leave in a hurry. So, I guarantee they left evidence behind. Proof that your daughter was there will be found—along with the body of a man connected to your brother and Tom Matthews. Now, your brother may be able to use his influence to weather the investigation and scandal, but do you really think that Calloway will buy that any of this is a coincidence? Your time working for him is over. Which not only makes you useless but a liability. Wonder what kind of solution Tom and the congressman have in store to remedy that?" Elle asked.

Denial was plain on the woman's face. "You're just trying to manipulate me."

"Manipulate you into what, exactly? If you're innocent, then what could we possibly be trying to do here?"

"You're after my brother, trying to use me to get to him."

"I don't care about your brother or you. Both of you are a means to an end to get to the man holding your leash."

"I work for the U.S. Government."

"Is that your defense for treason? Delusions of grandeur?"

"Fuck you."

"Hmmm, must have hit a nerve there. Don't worry, Kim. You don't have to tell me anything. Your phone should give me most of the information I need." Elle pulled out the phone. Kim lunged for it. Elle struck her with the flat of her hand, hitting the bridge of her nose. Eyes tearing up, she recoiled back into the seat with a cry and held her hands to her face. Moving fast, Elle wrapped cable ties around Kim's wrists and ran another one through the handle on the door. With the child lock engaged, there was nowhere for Kim to go.

"You may not want to struggle too much. It's going to tear up your skin and make your hands swell. We're going to be driving for a while, so the more you fight, the more pain you'll be in."

"Please, just let me go. I'll help you any way I can. I'm not the bad guy."

"Funny. You're the second person to say that to me this week. He was wrong, too."

Elle held the phone in front of Kim's face unlocking it before she could turn away. Going to the phone's call log, Elle took note of the last outgoing number. It was labeled Seth. She called her brother when she left HQ. The most recent call was received from a number that wasn't assigned to a contact. The call had lasted for twenty-five seconds.

Enough time to pass orders, but not enough time to get a fix on the caller. Turning the phone toward Kim, she asked, "What did Tom tell you?"

Pause. "It was a wrong number."

Gotcha, you son of a bitch. "Thank you, Kim."

"For what?"

"Giving me a direct link to Tom Matthews."

"I told you, it was a wrong number."

"Well, if you've been telling the truth, you have nothing to worry about." Elle didn't miss the change in the woman's breathing or the way she froze for a moment. Kim Daniels knew she was in a bad spot. She had to be questioning whether she could trust her brother, or Tom for that matter, to get her out of it.

After committing the numbers to memory, Elle turned off Bluetooth and Wi-Fi on the phone, then placed it in Airplane Mode before shutting it off. They would need to turn it back on later, but she didn't want it trying to find a network when they did.

Using the burner cell, Elle dialed Jack. "You guys on the road?"

"Yeah. We have all the gear, and we're on our way. It might take us a while since Eve drives like a little old lady," Jack said.

"I heard that!" Eve said in the background.

"Any updates?"

"The police haven't released any info to the public yet. So, all the news channels are just covering the activity at the scene now, but it won't be long before one of them runs the plates on the BMW and gets Kim's name. The police put out a BOLO for the Impala but haven't found it yet. The witnesses couldn't agree on whether it was green or blue. And the search grid is behind you. If no one takes any special interest in that car, you should be okay."

"Thanks, Jack. I have one more thing for you. Write down this number and tell me anything you can about it when you get here." Jack repeated the number to confirm it. Then, Elle said, "You guys be safe. See you soon." Hanging up, Elle turned her attention to Tex and Julian. "Do we have a first-aid kit in here somewhere?"

"There's one in the trunk. I think you can access the space by pulling the seats forward," Tex said.

Turning around, Elle saw that the rear seat was split into two parts. Shifting forward to get as much clearance as possible, she pulled on the backrest until it moved. There was a terrible smell coming from the trunk space, but she could see the first-aid kit. Grabbing it, she pushed the seat back into place. "Damn, did something die back there?"

"Probably. That's why I was able to talk the seller down from five grand to two," Tex said.

Elle just shook her head and shifted her attention to Julian. "Can you turn around and let me look at that?"

"I'll try. Pretty sure this seat is stuck as far forward as it goes. Beat the hell out of my knees just trying to get in."

Elle pulled out some cotton and alcohol swabs to clean to the wound. The blood had soaked Julian's shirt around the collar. There was a gash on the side of his head. It was shallow but, since head wounds bleed like crazy, it looked a lot worse than it was. As she cleaned the gash, Elle realized what must have caused the injury. It was a graze from a bullet. Her stomach lurched, and she fought to keep a straight face. Didn't matter, Julian knew. "It's nothing. I'll heal, but I'm pretty sure this shirt is trashed. Too bad. I thought it brought out the color of my eyes."

While she appreciated his effort at making light of the situation, she couldn't shake the anxiety. Everyone she cared about was in the line of fire. It wasn't just a figure of speech. And here she was, leading them into the flames. What would she do if they got burned?

CHAPTER 12

Thursday, 1530: Virginia Beach, Virginia

Three and a half hours later, they were in Virginia Beach. Elle had been reluctant to come to the area when Julian had suggested it, but she didn't have many options. And he'd presented a convincing proposal. Someplace they wouldn't be expected or stand out, with a spot to hold a hostage. Sold. However, now that she was there, she was having second thoughts.

The heavily populated area was home for Julian and his SEAL Team. He knew it like the back of his hand. But, more importantly, he knew how many different organizations practiced clandestine activities in the area. He knew what to say to pass off anything they did as a training event—at least long enough to buy them time to get clear of any local police involvement.

The sound of jets flying overhead reminded her of being in combat zones. But it seemed to be a common occurrence for the area, as no one seemed to pay them any mind. Traffic moved fast, with drivers weaving through the lanes around slower vehicles. They kept with the flow, eventually getting off the highway and working their way farther south through the city. Elle tensed when they drove right next to a military base. She caught glimpses of airfields and figured this was where all the jet noise came from. Julian, once again, read her mind.

"NAS Oceana, largest jet base on the east coast."

"Do we want to be this close?"

"You can't spit without hitting a base in this area. There's another one not far away. Lots of activity and vehicles around here. We can blend into the crowd and disappear."

Elle mulled that over. Tom undoubtedly had contacts in the military ranks, but would he activate his entire resource network or just those he needed for the search? Julian's connection to the area would increase the risk that someone would be watching for them here. But one thing was certain: they could disappear in plain sight. They were essentially anonymous. "How much longer?"

"About another fifteen minutes," Julian said.

He guided Tex through a few commercial areas to a long, winding road. Intersecting roads were farther and farther apart, and they were surrounded by more wooded areas. It was one hell of a channel. If this was the only way to get where they were going, Elle was liking their chances. Abruptly, their surroundings changed, and they were in a scene from a beach movie. The road ended at a traffic light, forcing them to turn south. The ocean to the east, sand and beach houses to their west. According to the signs, they were in a place called Sandbridge. This wasn't what she had pictured when Julian pitched it.

"Why didn't anyone tell me to bring my bathing suit?" Tex asked.

"Work first, play later, Tex," Elle said.

Pulling her knife, Elle grabbed the cable tie that attached Kim to the car door. The woman tried to tear away when she realized she was being touched but didn't have anywhere to go. Even that slight movement made her flinch in pain. She had been blindfolded and gagged for most of the ride. The moment her arms were released, she whimpered. The skin was raw and swollen where her wrists were still bound.

Julian directed them to a two-story beach house with a garage. It looked nice...except for the fact it had neighbors on both sides. Close neighbors. When they pulled into the driveway, Julian walked up to the garage and input a code in the keypad. The door opened, revealing an empty space. Tex drove the car inside, and Julian closed the door behind them.

Tex walked to the rear passenger side of the car and got Kim out. Elle stood and stretched her legs. They followed Julian through the attached garage and into a short hallway with a staircase and another door. This led to a room with a concrete floor and thick black acoustic tile on the walls and ceiling.

Tex whistled. "Who the hell lives here?"

"Me. Well, kinda," Julian said.

"What do you mean?"

"I'm going to sublet it from one of the guys who was on my team. He's doing a tour on the west coast now but doesn't want to give up the place since he plans on retiring here."

"Is there anything connecting you other than a verbal agreement?" Tex asked.

"Not that I'm aware of, and definitely nothing official. We were supposed to do the paperwork when I got back home from deployment, which would have been in a couple of weeks if I hadn't joined up with you guys."

"So, what's the story with this room?"

"Music room. He liked to unwind by beating the hell out of his drum set. Not exactly a popular pastime with neighbors, so he built this. Completely soundproof."

Elle ran her hand over the tile and smiled. *I stand corrected.* "Tex, go ahead and put Kim in the far corner. We'll rotate guard duty. Why don't you two go get cleaned up and check on Jack and Eve. I'll take the first shift with Kim."

The men closed the door behind them, and the sudden silence caused a ringing in her ears. Elle yanked the blindfold off the bound woman on the floor and then pushed the gag down. Kim squinted and looked around cautiously. She'd heard the discussion and knew she was in a soundproof room. That screaming was useless. But her expression said she was going to try, anyway.

"Before you do something foolish, I want you to think about one thing—if you ruin my plans, what do you think I'll do to you?"

"You're going to kill me, anyway."

"I could slit your throat right now. Would make things simpler. Dead or alive, it doesn't matter for what I have in mind. So, are you going to make it worthwhile to keep you alive?" Elle asked.

The color drained from Kim's face. "This is all your fault. If it hadn't been for you, none of this would have happened. Why couldn't you just stay away!"

"If you hadn't been so eager to get rid of your daughter, you wouldn't be here. Did you volunteer to be Tom's insider? Was pimping out Anne your idea?"

"Fuck you!"

"Do the traffickers help fund your image? The clothes, car, condo…seems a little on the high end for a government employee. Even one with your connections. If it wasn't for your brother, you'd have been investigated by our counterintelligence division months ago."

Kim was shaking, her face mottled with red splotches.

Elle sighed as she unclipped the knife from her jeans. Flipping open the blade, she walked over to her.

"What are you doing?!? Stop! You can't do this!"

Placing the blade against Kim's throat, Elle said, "Who's going to stop me? You know how I operate. And I have nothing to lose." Applying pressure, Elle watched the fear in her captive's eyes turn to panic and then desperation.

Elle pierced the skin on her neck.

As the first rivlet of blood ran down her neck, Kim's resistance broke. "Stop! I'll cooperate! Please. Tell me what you want!"

Elle pulled back, wiped the knife on Kim's pants and put it away. Then, she stood, turned, and hit record on the cell phone hidden inside her jacket. Leaning against the wall, she asked, "I want everything you know about Tom Matthews and his operations."

"I can't. He'll kill me."

"So, die now or die later. Sounds like it's in your best interest to delay your death sentence as much as possible. Maybe even get clear of it altogether—if Tom dies."

"Are you saying you'll let me go if I help you?" Kim asked.

"Tom's my target, Kim," Elle said.

"What about my daughter?

"The odds of survival for both of you go up if you give me Tom."

"I swear, I didn't know Matthews was involved until a few months ago."

"But you've been a mole for your brother for years."

Kim's head bowed, but she nodded.

"Keep going."

"At first, Seth didn't ask me for anything specific. It was just him keeping tabs on what Calloway and the directorate were up to. He's a Congressman and on the oversight committee. He would have known about the stuff I was giving him eventually, anyway. So it wasn't a big deal."

"Keep going, Kim."

"But then you got captured. Seth demanded immediate updates. When those weren't detailed enough, he told me to get him everything in your file. I told him I didn't have clearance for that. He didn't care. He told me to get it no matter what…or else. I gave him everything I could. And things were quiet for a while. I thought it was over, but then you came back to work."

"He gave you new orders?"

"Not Seth. Matthews. He threatened me. And my daughter."

"Let me guess, he was going to go public about your daughter if you didn't get him what he wanted."

"I thought she was going to boarding school. Seth set it up, and I signed the paperwork and put her on a train. It was perfect." Kim started sobbing. "But then I got a call. A man told me he could prove that I sold Anne...to sex traffickers. The papers I signed ...weren't real. He sent me pictures...

"Why didn't you go to the police?"

"The man told me that Anne wouldn't be ...touched...as long as I cooperated. But if I refused or called the police, he'd let them do whatever they wanted to her."

"What did your brother say when you told him?"

"Seth told me to just do what they said, and everything would be fine. He would take care of the police. As long as we stuck with our story and kept the information coming, we had nothing to worry about."

More to the point, Seth Daniels would have nothing to worry about. Whether he was in on the plan or not, it was apparent the Congressman was more concerned with keeping his position than finding his niece. In one move, Tom had everything he needed to control a sitting congressman and gain access to the most sensitive information at the CIA.

"Why didn't you ask Calloway for help?"

"I was scared he wouldn't believe me. The people who took Anne deposited money in my account every week to make me look guilty. Seth said if I got fired...we'd both be dead."

"So, Tom got your brother to set the trap and then blackmailed you into doing his dirty work."

"It's not like that! Tom trapped Seth, too. He forced us to work for him. What choice did we have?"

Elle didn't bother responding to that BS. "What did you do for Tom, specifically?"

"I had to get access to your operations."

"I want everything, Kim. Now is not the time to hold back."

"After you escaped the ambush at your house, Matthews lost it. He demanded I find you. But no one knew anything. After you broke into my house, I told Seth. I didn't think he'd call Matthews. He loves Anne. He does."

Elle very much doubted that.

Kim began sobbing. "But Seth must have called him. When I was on the way to my house, Matthews called. He was pissed that the police were already on the way and told me to get rid of them as soon as possible. Then he would have his people come to inspect the house for me."

"If we hadn't grabbed you, Tom's people would have. He wanted to make sure you weren't holding anything back."

"What do you mean?"

"You were literally the closest person to Calloway, the man with all the answers. He would never believe that you were being completely honest about what you knew. He was going to force your cooperation."

Kim paled. "But I told him everything I knew."

"More to the point, you told him everything you thought he wanted to hear. One thing I will agree with Tom on is that you know more than you think you do."

"I don't! I'm not lying!"

"Didn't say that. I want you to walk me through every interaction you had with Tom. Exactly what he said, how he said it, and any other details you can remember—no matter how small."

***

Elle's pulse pounded in her ears, but she kept a straight face as she sat quietly processing the information that she had just pulled out of Kim Daniels. She had reframed her questions several times and asked for clarification on things she already knew to verify that the answers Kim was giving her were true. She had a lead. Now she needed to run it to ground.

There was no sound to warn her in the sound proof room, so Elle jumped when the door opened.

Tex stood on the other side. "The kids are here, they grabbed some food on the way, and we got all our gear set up." His eyes narrowed when he saw the thin streak of blood that had begun clotting on Kim's neck. "Figured you could use a break."

"Perfect. Thanks, Tex," Elle said. She walked past him and up the stairs to the second floor, which led to an open concept kitchen and living room. She could smell fries and saw Eve in the kitchen unpacking bags of Chick-fil-A. Her stomach growled, but the food wasn't what was most important to her right now. "Jack, please tell me you have something on that phone number."

Sitting on the floor in the dining area, Jack shoved a waffle fry in his mouth and shrugged. "I did what I could,

Elle. I was piggybacking off people's hot spots while we were on the way. Luckily, it's getting more common for cars to have Wi-Fi, but there were still lots of dead spots, which made this a big challenge. On the bright side, it would be a nightmare for anyone to try and track me."

"So, what did you find out?"

"The phone was activated a week ago. And has been pinging off a tower on the eastern shore of Virginia. That's the best I can do."

"Not yet, it isn't. I want you and Eve to overlay your data on a map of the area, then add in private airport locations."

Julian walked in from a hallway likely leading to bedrooms. He was freshly showered and changed. The wound on his head already looked better. "Did Kim give you something?"

"She's too self-absorbed to truly pay attention to others, but something she said jumped out at me. In their first direct conversation, Tom told her not to bother asking for help because no one would be able to get close to him: 'not even a bird could fly by without me knowing about it.' The first part is standard scare tactic bullshit, but the line about the bird seems off. What if it means he controls airspace?"

"That's a lot of what-ifs, Elle."

"I know, but it fits. Tom can't come into the country through a regular port of entry. The agency would be all over him the second he was ID'd. So, he would need to stay outside territorial waters or use a private airfield or port. If he picked the right one, he could make it his base of operations and have multiple avenues of escape. A private airfield would also give him the luxury of being able to use the control tower as an early warning system. If any aircraft were sent to investigate or as part of a raid force, he'd know about it."

Elle hovered behind Eve as she took the information Jack pulled for her and layered it over a map of the eastern shore of Virginia. After studying the results, Eve said, "It looks like we have four possibilities. All around the Cape Charles area. I'll do some more research and see what I can find out about each location."

"Let me know the second you find anything anomalous. Even if it seems trivial."

"Of course. We're on it, Elle."

"The armed kidnapping of a congressman's sister is the top story. It's gone national. The heat is going to be really turning up now," Jack said.

"It was inevitable. And, if we play our hand right, exactly what we need."

"We're going to need to be ready to move. I'll check our gear and the vehicles," Julian said.

Jack, is there anything around here you can tap into to give us as much of an early warning as possible if we're found?"

"Pretty sure every other house has a doorbell camera or something. If they haven't locked down their Wi-Fi, it's mine."

"Do it. But make sure you cover your tracks. We need to be invisible."

"I'm going to pretend I didn't hear that."

"What's the setup like here?" Elle asked Julian.

"We have a bedroom and a bathroom at the end of each hallway. No furniture, but the water and electricity are on. All the gear is over there," Julian said, pointing to a corner in the living room.

"Alright. This is too exposed. Pick whichever room has the most concealment from prying eyes, and let's move the weapons there. I'll leave you to handle them. After you check everything, get some rest. You'll be relieving Tex, so he can get some sleep, too. I'll nap until we have a location."

Nodding, Julian grabbed the bags with their small armory and moved down the hall.

Elle watched him for a moment before finding the bathroom and cleaning up as much as she could. She then made her way into a small bedroom. It was just an empty box with a tile floor, but it would do. Sleep wasn't a likely scenario for her, but she could at least try to rest and clear her mind.

A battle was looming.

CHAPTER 13

Thursday, 1800: Virginia Beach, Virginia

Here's what we have so far, Elle. I created files for each of the airfields but ranked them based on probability. It's a coin toss for the top spot, so I'll go alphabetically. Earth Airport is up first."

"Seriously? Who the hell named it that?" Tex asked.

"Unknown. It's owned by a holding company based in the Cayman Islands. The property was purchased two years ago via wire transfer. It's registered for private use, but no names."

"I'm liking where this is heading, Eve. Keep going," Elle said.

Eve flipped around her laptop. On the screen was an overhead satellite image showing an airfield right next to the Chesapeake Bay, surrounded by trees. A single road went to the airport. It had two small hangers, several buildings, and a control tower. "This image is a few years old, but we found a contract from a local company that specializes in fences. So, it's probable the entire airfield has been secured with privacy fencing. Jack is digging into the utilities to see if that can help us narrow things down further."

"Good. Jack, keep at it. What's next?"

"The second airfield has changed hands three times in the last year. It's registered for use as an import and export business, and the license was just renewed four days ago. I found some conspiracy theories online about it being attached to organized crime. Most of it's ridiculous, but I did find a connection to an unsolved murder. A blogger who did a compelling piece on the place went missing. They found his body in the bay last year."

"Show me," Elle said.

Again, Eve showed Elle an image of the airfield in question. It was in a more rural area and larger than the first. It had four hangers, some smaller support buildings, and a tower. There was one access road, but the fields surrounding it were open, and there didn't appear to be any security gates.

"What else do you have?" Elle asked.

"The other two locations seem pretty straightforward. I couldn't find anything that jumped out at me. They're privately owned businesses, both registered and with multiple listed points of contact. They seem to cater to private pilots and chartered flights. From what I can tell, they do fairly regular business and have for years." Eve toggled through the images of the last two locations as she spoke so Elle could see them. Nothing jumped out at her, and she couldn't imagine Tom wanting to be so open. Unless it was a front for his operations, but it just didn't seem right.

"Jack, focus your efforts on the first location."

"Why that one? I thought the murder pointed right at Tom's people," Eve asked.

"It's the exposure and timeline that doesn't fit. Murder is Tom's style, but the sloppy operations aren't. That and the lack of a perimeter fence or access to the water for a secondary escape route."

Jack was typing furiously. Elle moved behind him and watched lines of code flying across the screen. Whatever he was doing, she couldn't follow it.

"Eve, what's the latest in the news?"

"The kidnapping is the top story everywhere. Because of her brother, it's a federal case. They're calling it politically motivated, with both sides pointing fingers at the extremists on the other. A grainy video of the incident is circulating, but it's tough to make out anything other than the color and type of vehicles involved and movement between the cars. Congressman Daniels is supposed to give a press conference in an hour."

"Any official statement from his office?"

"The usual. The Congressman is deeply concerned about his sister and is working closely with law enforcement to find her—"

"Whoo!" Jack yelled.

Interrupting everyone and causing Eve to jump.

"Sorry," he said to Eve mostly, "but I'm in. I've accessed the power grid, and Earth airfield is operating twenty-four seven. I crossed-checked flight plans filed with the FAA and confirmed that no planes have arrived or departed in the last couple of days, but the power draw didn't change.

So, unless they're literally flying under the radar, there's no reason for them not to shut things down at night that I can find."

"Great work, Jack. I agree that's our target. Tex, let's go do some recon to see what we're dealing with. We'll take the Civic since it will be less alerting. Go check on Julian to make sure he's good to stay with our guest. Eve, we need to know everything that happens at that press conference. Be alert for any details that could tell us their plans or what leads they have. Any clue, no matter how small, could be clutch for us. Jack, keep digging to see what other contracting or support services have been used at that airfield."

Tex returned to the room and said, "Julian's good. Eve, I told him you'd check in periodically."

"No problem. Anything else?"

"Just keep digging for more information and keep your heads down. If this is Tom's base of operations...we're in for one hell of a fight. We'll need as much information as we can get."

"Where are we starting?" Tex asked.

"The waterline. I want to know how easy it is to approach and access the airfield from there. And if they have a pier set up."

"Looks like there are breakwaters set up all through there. May be a way in via the beach, but those could easily mask intrusion alarms or cameras until we were right on top of them," Tex said.

"Agreed. I think we're going to need a boat. The town of Arlington, just to the south of the airfield, is too close. If we're right about this place, Tom will have eyes out watching for strangers in the area. Eve, what can you tell me about the city of Cape Charles to the north?"

"Small community. Looks nice. I saw several references to seafood festivals to bring in tourists."

"Catering to tourists helps us. Anyone on Tom's payroll would have a hard time telling who's who in a crowd of visitors. As long as we don't draw attention to ourselves, it's our best option. We go in, rent a boat, and sail down past the target area."

"Aye, aye, Captain."

"Let's get moving, smartass."

They returned to the garage and got back into the Civic. Elle wanted the SUV that Eve and Jack had arrived in off the grid as long as possible. Pulling out of the garage, Elle felt her tension rise. The bright beach scene in front of her felt like a trap waiting to spring. She scrutinized their surroundings, looking for any signs that could denote trouble. People were out riding bikes or walking their dogs. It was a beautiful, sunny day. Nothing seemed out of place.

Except us.

"This is a really nice area. After all this shit with Tom is over, think Julian would let me crash here for a bit? I could use a vacation," Tex said.

Elle chuckled. "Vacation from what, cupcake?"

"I've put in at least ten minutes of labor today; pretty sure my union contract states I max out at five. So, I should get overtime and paid vacation days from this."

"I'll make a note of it," Elle said. Once they turned west and left the beach area, Elle relaxed a little more. The tree-lined road felt more secure. On the flip side, this road would be a perfect place to set up an ambush. The trees lining both sides of the two-lane road would provide concealment for just about anything.

"It'll be about an hour before we get there, Tex. We need to blend in as best we can. The longer we drive around with the fake temp plates, the higher the chance we get burned."

"If we switched plates in an area like this, it'd be reported within a couple of hours."

"Yeah, a short-term gain, but it would increase our heat-state in the long run. So, what's your plan?"

"Still working on it. But it's going to get messy no matter what we do." Elle paused for a moment before adding, "Mike, you need to know…some of what's coming; you need to let me do it on my own."

"I'm not having this conversation with you. Again. We're a team. We're in this together, all the way."

"Even if it means killing innocents?"

Tex had no response.

"There's going to be collateral damage. Tom doesn't care who gets placed in the line of fire. But you do."

"And you don't?"

"I can't. Not if I want to end this."

"Come on, Elle. There's got to be another way. If you start killing indiscriminately, what makes you different from Tom?"

"Maybe I'm not. Maybe the only difference is that I don't want it to happen. But if it comes down to me getting to Tom or the lives of strangers—I know what I'm going to choose. You need to stay as far away from that as possible."

"There's no coming back from that. If you kill bystanders, you'll be the criminal they think you are."

"They won't be bystanders, but you're right. There's no going back. This will be mutually assured destruction. Even if I kill him, he wins. If I'm alive, I'll be considered a criminal. But, at least he'll be dead, and you will all be safe."

"Drop the martyr bullshit, Elle. You're going to find a way to get the job done and get clear of this. Period. Anything else would be a copout, and that's not you. So, stop slacking off and get your head back in the game."

They rode in silence for a while. Elle kept turning the options over in her head, but her way ahead seemed locked in. Mutually assured destruction. Tex was overestimating her—that's the conclusion she came to. That faith could get them all killed. Unless she could get them all clear. They were only targets because of her.

As they started making their way across the miles of bridges and tunnels that crossed the Chesapeake Bay from Virginia Beach to the peninsula of the Eastern Shore, they found themselves surrounded by water. The view was incredible, and Elle allowed her thoughts to clear and just enjoy the ocean.

Her reverie was broken when the driver's seat creaked as Tex shifted his weight.

Automatically checking the side mirror, she asked, "What's wrong?"

"Another one of those damn tunnels is coming up."

"So?"

"What do you mean, so? We're about to drive underwater.

Doesn't that seem a little crazy to you? One leak, and it's over."

"Going to go out on a limb and say that we're in good shape, Tex. Relax."

"I'll relax when we see the sun again."

Elle shook her head but took another look at the tunnel. He had a point, but she refused to show it. Taking a deep breath, she leaned back in the seat and waited to hit the surface again. The vehicles ahead of them slowed as drivers started heading back up toward the sunlight, causing an accordion effect, but they were back on the bridge in no time.

There was moderate traffic, making Elle uneasy. Unless any tails got right on their ass and introduced themselves, it would be almost impossible to identify if they were being followed.

Elle studied the drivers behind them through the side mirror, watching for cars drifting in the lanes or any other demeanor hits. The closer they got to Tom, the higher the risk. He was a piece of shit, but Tom knew what he was doing. They could trigger a response at any time. Reaching the Eastern Shore, they kept moving north.

As soon as they paid the toll and drove off the bridge, it was like they were in a different place altogether. Beautiful beaches, wetlands, and forested areas gave way to an RV park and hotels. From there, the area was interspersed with patches of luxury living and poverty. Homes with million-dollar views and new construction were hidden behind tree lines, while the main road had faded, hand-painted signs for lobster rolls or bright-yellow fireworks stores scattered every quarter of a mile or so. It was like the area had an identity crisis.

Following the signage to Cape Charles, they arrived in the quaint, postcard-like town. It was right on the bay and looked peaceful. In a few minutes, they managed to navigate through to the small marina. There was a well-maintained boathouse and a sign out front advertising rentals and chartered boats. The man behind the counter was a walking stereotype. Early sixties, sturdy, tattoos covering both arms, wearing jeans and a T-shirt—ex-military to be sure.

Tex arranged the rental, making small talk with the retired Navy Boatswain's Mate, while Elle "browsed" the shop to give her better angles to watch through the windows for anyone approaching. Leaving the boathouse, they walked to the next slip and jumped into a small fishing boat. It was an older model but impeccably maintained. Perfect.

As they maneuvered through the marina out into the bay, Elle couldn't help but wish they were there under different circumstances. The sun made the water shine, and there was a soft breeze. Sitting at the bow, she forced herself to focus on the task at hand. This wasn't a pleasure cruise. Watching the coastline, Elle hunted for any clue of how Tom might have set up shop.

How would I do it?

Pulling out her burner, Elle used the device to see what Wi-Fi networks were discoverable. Surprisingly, even on the water, she picked up several. All the signals were locked down and seemed to be connected to businesses. Minutes passed, and the coastline appeared to be the same.

"Doesn't look like there are any piers down this way. The water looks too shallow. Any pier would have to jut out pretty far. That's probably not authorized, and they'd have to pull out a breakwater to make it happen."

Elle sighed. "Yeah. Now the question is whether that's a good thing for us or not."

Using the phone's GPS, she estimated they were approaching the airfield. If she hadn't been looking at the screen, she might have missed the moment the signal dropped. Being on the water, dead zones were expected, but chances were high this one was manmade. "Cell phone jammer. We're here."

"What do you want me to do?" Tex asked.

"Keep going, don't change speed or course." Elle moved to sit next to Tex and shifted her position so her back was to the shoreline. "I need your eyes. Anyone watching us will see a couple talking to each other. Tell me what you see."

"Thick forest, and not much space between that and the water. There's a break coming up in the trees. I can see a fence. Eight-foot tall, chain-link, razor wire on top." He paused. "We have a camera, Elle."

"Act natural. We're vulnerable right now. Any security needs to write us off."

In one fluid movement, Tex wrapped his arm around her, pulling her body in closer to his. Elle stiffened instinctually but told herself to relax. He bowed his head, giving the impression that he was kissing her. Rationally, she understood what he was doing. If they looked like a couple more interested in each other than the surroundings, it would buy them time. But she was still thrown by the sudden intimacy.

"Relax, Elle. You should be honored that I even deigned to allow you to get this close to me."

Elle laughed, which released most of her anxiety. "Next time, bust out the Tic-Tacs first." She put her arms around him so they could maintain the ruse while she spoke into his ear, "We need to figure out how far south their cameras reach and where the blind spots are."

"It's a dome camera mounted on a light post. I can't tell where it's oriented, but it probably has multi-directional coverage."

"Do we have anything we can work with?"

"Looks like they've trimmed back the trees on the south side, but it's still pretty thick back there. Even if they have infrared, cameras would have a hard time penetrating that. But so would we. If I remember from the overhead images, it's marshy in there too."

"They may have thought that was enough of a deterrent. In most situations, they would've been right."

"How much longer before we turn around—shit," Tex cursed.

"What is it?"

"Jet skis. Two of them. They're parked beside one of the breakwaters."

"Riders?"

"I don't see any movement yet. But those will give them a lot more reach, and they can go faster than we can."

"Start angling away from the coast. Let's get some distance between us without making it look like we're intentionally turning away."

Angling to the southwest, they rode in silence for a while. The new angle allowed Elle to use her peripheral vision to watch the coastline. No one was pursuing them. At least not that she could see. Given how much effort Tom was putting into killing her, it was a safe bet they hadn't triggered any alarms. Tex was right, the jet skis could overtake them, and they'd be at an extreme disadvantage in a fight. No way Tom wouldn't jump on the chance.

Shifting back to sitting side-by-side, Elle said, "The sun is setting. Go ahead and start making the turn. Keep it wide to keep us further away. We may be far enough out now to be off their radar, but let's not chance it. We need to be damn near invisible now."

"Want another look? We could go full redneck and tromp through the swamp."

"I think we're out of time and moves. There's no plausible reason for us to be in the swamp and higher chances for us to leave a trail that could alert them if they do regular patrols. The next time we come here, we need to be going in. It'll have to be quick and aggressive. We'll have one shot."

"I'm your huckleberry. We coming back tonight?"

"No. Tomorrow. We have another big problem to deal with first."

"The congressman?"

"Yeah. With the Congressman still in play, so are the Secret Service and all the legitimate law enforcement guys thinking they're working a high-profile kidnapping case. We can't tangle with them and Tom's mercenaries at the same time. It's going to be complicated enough to do it consecutively."

"How are you going to deal with Dirty Daniels?"

"Dirty Daniels?"

"Feels wrong calling that douche 'Congressman.'" Smiling, he added, "How do you think ol' Double D will handle getting his ass kicked. I bet he cries like a bitch."

"You'll get the chance to see for yourself. Let's stir up some trouble."

CHAPTER 14

Thursday, 2000: Virginia Beach, Virginia

The sun had set by the time Elle and Tex returned to the beach house in Sandbridge. The drive back had been uneventful, so Elle had plenty of time to think. She had an idea of what she wanted to do but not how to make it happen. There were too many unknowns. She needed more information.

"Eve, does the congressman have a place in D.C?" Elle asked.

"Yes, he has a condo not far from the National Mall."

"Good. That should work. What did you learn from the press conference?"

"The search for Kim is focused here in Virginia, and the prevailing theory is that she was taken to put pressure on the Congressman—to throw a vote or something. The police have ID'd one of the guys who was tailing Kim as a local gang member, and they assume that the second shooter was part of the same gang. The media is spinning it as a kidnap-for-hire scheme, but their suspect list reads like a bad movie plot. The guy they ID'd is in the hospital, but he's not talking. They have blood and fingerprints from the second guy, so they expect to make another arrest soon."

"More local hires. They'll be dead before the night is over."

"Should we stake out the hospital? See who shows up?" Julian asked.

"It'll be another minion. We need to stay with the biggest asset Tom has. That's how we fracture his network. Anything else, Eve?"

"No. Congressman Daniels spoke for a brief moment. He seemed sincere when he said that he hopes to find his sister soon."

"Of course, he did. He's a politician. He lies for a living. But, truthfully, he does need her. Even if he doesn't care about her, he definitely cares about his access to the CIA. Someone with her placement isn't easy to come by. Let alone turn."

"I still can't believe he could just stand by while traffickers have his niece." Eve paused for a moment. "Do you think they'll kill Anne now that we know?"

"As fucked up as it is, she's safer right now than she would be if we had pulled her out."

"How can you say that?"

"Tom needs her alive to keep the Daniels siblings in line. If she were to be killed, he'd lose his leverage. They could go on the offensive or come up with a patsy to take the fall and get clear of everything. If we had rescued her, she'd have gone back to her mother, and then they would have disappeared—permanently. Tom would have made sure of it." Elle shifted topics. "How many different systems can you break into at one time, Jack?"

"I'm not sure if I should be insulted or intrigued, Elle. What kind of systems are you talking about?"

"Anything with a display."

"Where?"

"Eve, where's the next press conference happening?"

"FBI headquarters, tomorrow morning."

"Jack?"

"If I had a week to plan and work on it, maybe. But something tells me that won't work for you."

"You'd be correct. Okay, so we make Congressman Daniels stay someplace we want him to be. Somewhere the Secret Service won't object to."

"How the hell are we supposed to get him to go where we want? His security detail will be on high alert going anywhere they haven't cleared, and they'll pack him up at the first sign of trouble, Elle."

"So, we keep him someplace they've already cleared."

"Where?"

"His residence. And we make sure there's plenty to keep him occupied while he's there."

"What do you mean?"

"Jack, I want you to get started on accessing the digital traffic signage—and any other displays you think you can get control of. I want to be able to flash a message of our choosing on as many screens around D.C. as possible. You've got until six tomorrow morning."

"Traffic signs shouldn't be hard. I'll start there. I'll let you know what else I can come up with," Jack said as he started typing.

"Eve, it's press release time."

"Huh?"

"Take everything we know about Daniels, and write it up. Highlight his part in what happened to his niece, his connection to Nash, and the trafficking ring. And then include the dirty cops, and how he's been abusing his sister's position at the CIA for his own gain. Tex, could you relieve Julian? I have another job for him."

"Sure thing."

Handing Tex one of the tablets, Elle added, "Got some homework for you, too. While you're down there, find the anonymous tip lines for every news outlet in the D.C. area and the emails for whichever politicians are trending."

He let out a whistle. "You're about to create a shit storm," Tex said.

"What better way to get law enforcement off our backs and split Tom's resources than making Daniels breaking news everywhere. Politicians on both sides of the aisle will be screaming for answers, which will elevate this nationally."

"I hope they catch his reaction on camera. Just wish I could be there to see his house of cards come tumbling down."

"You may get your wish."

"What do you mean?" Tex followed her into the kitchen.

"I need Tom to believe I'm in D.C. orchestrating the play against Daniels, and I need to force him to act. You're his next best shot at getting to me—which means he'll shift from a kill to a capture mission. Less likelihood of bloodshed, and higher probability of him expending significant resources to catch you."

"So, what I'm hearing is that you're turning me into the world's prettiest decoy."

Elle snorted. "Beauty's in the eye, cupcake, but, yes—you're part of the diversion. You need to take this seriously. You cannot get captured. Tom will send in professional muscle. This is going to be dangerous. If he gets his hands on you, it's game over."

"I'm not going to let that happen. You sure this is the play? I don't like the idea of leaving you on your own."

"Julian can back me up, and he'll be able to watch out for Eve and Jack if anything goes sideways. We're all targets on Tom's hit list, which is why it needs to be either you or Julian that goes—it has to be someone who can handle themselves. But I can't count on Julian's presence to get the reaction I want. Tom knows how close we are. For you, he'll send out his best players. Are you ready to take that on?"

"I'd be insulted if he didn't. Not going to let you down, Elle."

A sudden burning sensation hit the back of her eyes. She turned away, heading for the fridge, so she could blink and recover. Elle grabbed a bottle of water. She hadn't realized how thirsty she was until the first sip. She ended up downing the whole thing.

"Between the sun and humidity, you can get dehydrated pretty quickly," Julian said as he made his way over to her.

"The sun definitely feels more intense here. But we spent

a lot of time on the water so that amplified the effects. How's our guest?"

"I think she's given up. She's not even crying anymore. Just sitting there looking broken."

"Can't say I feel sorry. How about you?"

"Ready to do something other than babysitting."

"Good. I need you to go shopping."

"Not what I had in mind. What do you need?"

"Supplies. I know it's late, but I'm hoping things will still be open since it's a tourist destination. I don't want to take the vehicles out again until we have to, but I noticed a store up the road. Since you've been here before and less likely to be on anyone's hit list, you're the best option for getting some supplies without drawing attention."

"Groceries?"

"Gear. Going to go a little MacGyver here. I need tools, duct tape, flashlights, plastic bags or saran wrap, vanilla frosting, putty, anything with cheap circuitry, digital clocks, batteries, and water shoes."

"That's one hell of an interesting list."

"Get what you can, even if it's travel-sized shit. And a notepad and pencils. If you see anything else that may be good for a raid, feel free to grab it."

Julian laughed. "Not the kind of list that comes to mind when I think raid, but I'll do my best. What's your plan?"

"Need to see what I have to work with first."

"Something tells me you're not kidding. Okay, I'll be back as soon as I can."

Impulse made her reach out and grab his arm as he started to move away. She didn't trust the quiet, and it was making her edgy. Glancing at Eve and Jack to make sure they weren't watching, Elle leaned closer and said, "Be careful, Julian. If anything feels wrong, get yourself clear. Don't try to come back for us. If you don't return in the next ninety minutes, we'll assume you're in the wind and that we have company. I'll draw them away, and Tex will get Eve and Jack out."

"This isn't goodbye, Elle."

She felt a swell of emotion building. Unwilling to name it, Elle closed the distance between them and said, "Just in case it is." She kissed him. It felt perfect. She didn't understand why, but she no longer cared. The warmth of the kiss soon turned to heat, and she broke away.

He held her close a moment before pulling back and saying, "You're not getting off the hook that easily. Going to take more than a crazy ex-spy to push me away."

Depends on which ex-spy you're talking about.

"Stay frosty."

Smiling, he said, "See you soon."

Today had already been a roller coaster ride. And it wasn't over. Moving back to stand behind Eve and Jack, she drank a second bottle of water as she watched them work. A year ago, she didn't know who they were. Now, they were family, who had stood by her through hell and back. The idea of them being in harm's way, again, because of her—was unacceptable.

This would end tomorrow. One way or the other.

"How are we looking?" Elle said, breaking the silence.

"Just need a few more minutes, Elle. Then I'll be ready for you to review it," Eve said.

Jack kept typing as he said, "Got the traffic signs easy enough, so I took that line of thought a step further and accessed the displays at Union Station, Dulles, and BWI, too. Anyone traveling will see whatever you want them to."

"Nice work, Jack. How long until you're in those systems?"

"Huh? Oh, I'm already in. I was on a roll, so I kept going. Did you know Target has its own Wi-Fi for their stores? Really nice of them. All the display devices in the electronics section are attached to it...." With a few final keystrokes, Jack added, "And now they're mine, too."

"Alright, Mr. Wizard, how many screens does that give us?"

"About four hundred. Give or take depending on what's operational."

"No matter what happens, I need you to make damn sure you can't be tracked. If that means we only get our message out once, so be it. Once it's out there, it's out there."

"I know the deal, Elle. I've got as many protocols, and layers of security set up as I can. The second anything trips, I'll sever the connection. What do you want me to say?"

"That Congressman Seth Daniels gave his niece to traffickers and covered it up."

"Subtle. I like it." Jack started typing.

"Eve, you ready?"

"I think so. Never thought I'd be writing anything with the intent of giving it to the media. Feels weird." Eve handed the laptop to Elle.

Sitting on the floor next to Eve, she started scanning through the press release. All the key points were there, but

Elle adjusted the verbiage to have a more salacious angle just to make sure they had everyone's attention. After giving it a final read-through, she handed the laptop back to Eve. "Good job. Tex will have a list of email addresses for you soon. And I want you to include an attachment." Pulling the cell phone out of her pocket, she handed it to Eve. "There's a voice recording on here. Let's get it downloaded and have Jack clean it up so the metadata can't be traced back to us."

"No problem. What is it?" Eve asked.

"Kim Daniels's full confession and details on her brother's involvement with Tom," Elle said.

"Oh, wow. Did you record your interrogation? Sweet! Why didn't you tell us?" Jack asked.

"Didn't want to distract you from what you were doing. We were on a time crunch. Eve, feel free to see if there's anything more we can learn. Jack, once Tex brings up the email addresses—you know what to do. The press release and this attachment have to be untraceable.-Keep us invisible. If I know Tom, you're going to have your hands full soon. Don't let your guard down for a second," Elle said.

"Yeah, yeah, I got it," Jack said.

Elle left them and walked down the stairs to their makeshift holding cell. She banged on the door three times before she opened it, so Tex wasn't taken by surprise. He was propped up against the wall across from Kim. The tablet was on his lap, and it looked like he was surfing Twitter.

"At least tell me you don't follow the Kardashians," Elle said.

"They understand my burden. Everyone thinks I'm just a pretty face, too," Tex handed her the tablet. "Got all the emails you wanted. What's next?"

"It's time to be rid of our extra baggage," Elle said, looking at Kim.

She winced but otherwise didn't react.

"Where to?"

"We're taking her straight to Calloway. Do not pass go. Do not collect two hundred dollars."

"I like it, but can't we use her as bait? That would kick things up."

"She still is. If you were looking for us, where would you keep constant eyes?

"Headquarters."

"Exactly. In one move, we meet several goals and send Tom's network into chaos. Getting eyes on both you and Kim will cause a breakdown. They won't know where the priority is, so they will wait for direction. It will cause them to split resources while they wait for backup. That will buy you a window of time to get in and out after handing Kim over to the Agency. Wait to call Calloway's direct line until you're right there, just in case."

"If I were them, I'd have an ambush set up to intercept us before we made it to HQ."

"Probably. But Tom wants you both alive. If you die, he loses leverage. That gives you an advantage. And you know the area better than they do. We need to time your arrival for midday tomorrow. Lots of activity. I say use the visitor traffic to either Kryptos or Langley Park to blend in. But this part of the op will be all you. Run it how you see fit."

"What's my timeline?"

"We'll keep up the watch rotation and sleep and do gear prep between watches. I'm going to send Eve and Jack to bed soon so they can get back to it at 0500. But I'm going to get them started on one more task before they go to sleep: find Anne Daniels. When you get to HQ, you'll not only need to get Kim inside without being caught, but you have to convince Calloway to give you support to save the girl. It's not going to be easy, Mike. Are you ready for this?"

Tex gave her a penetrating look. "Tell me this is really necessary, Elle. Promise me that you aren't just trying to get rid of me so you can go on some suicide run at this guy."

"It's necessary. It would be suicide to make a run at Tom without your help. I'd never put you in the crosshairs if there was another way. We can't do an assault on the airfield with just us, and we can't call in the cavalry without alerting Tom that we've found him. He's too well connected, and he'd be gone before any assault team arrived. If he thinks our focus is on taking out his Daniels connections, we have the chance to end this."

"Okay. I distract Tom's boys and make them look like chumps, drop off Kim, get Calloway to back a rescue mission. Then what?"

"If you have a location for Anne by then, that takes priority. The sooner you get to her, the better her survival chances. If we don't have it yet, make your way over to Seth Daniels' house. The press will be camped out on his lawn by then, which will have Secret Service and the local police on high alert. Find a clever way to make sure that the Congressman knows that his sister is in custody. He should already know about her confession implicating him in treason. Feel free to rub that in, too."

"Let me guess. You want Daniels to call Tom and cry for help."

"Repeatedly. Think you can do it?"

"Make that little bitch piss his pants and run off crying? With pleasure."

"Stay on high alert until you know it's all over. I don't know how often Tom's minions check-in, so it's possible that they won't know their meal ticket is gone even after I take out Tom. Use the safehouse in Woodbridge once you're done playing with Daniels to regroup and plan. I'll have Eve and Jack go straight there after they kick things off in the morning. Julian and I will meet you when it's over tomorrow night."

"Okay. I'll refine my plans while I'm babysitting. When should I expect you or Julian to relieve me?"

"I sent Julian off for some supplies. When he gets back, we need to get our shit squared away. Once we're done, I'll have him come and relieve you. If you want to go get started with your prep, I've got this."

Tex got to his feet and approached Elle. He studied her face for a while before he wrapped his arms around her. "Don't even think about not coming back. I'm not joking. I will hunt you down in hell just to kick your ass if you mess this up."

"Would never dream of making things easier for you." Then, reluctantly, she pulled back. "Go get ready."

He looked like he wanted to say something, but she didn't want to draw out the moment. "We can do this, Mike. It's going to work."

Nodding, he squeezed her shoulder and walked out.

This was a lot harder than she had anticipated. *Find a distraction.*

"Ready for another road trip, Kim? I know you don't want to leave, but, hey, all good things must come to an end."

Kim just kept staring into space.

"You might as well drop the act. You can't play us. In fact, you may want to consider that our way is the only way you and your daughter don't end up dead or tortured."

"All I had to do was cooperate," Kim said to no one in particular. "And no one would have ever known. Anne would be safe. Now, they're going to do horrible things to her, and you ruined all our lives. For what? For your revenge. You aren't any different than Tom Matthews."

"If you want to blame me, go ahead. I won't lose any sleep over it. But don't for one second think that Anne would have ever tasted freedom again. You left your daughter in their hands for two years. She has seen too much, knows too many secrets. If they don't kill her—she'll be sold overseas and be as good as dead."

"You don't know that!"

"I do."

"Please, don't do this. There has to be another way."

"If I were you, I'd focus on helping us rescue Anne. Might win you some sympathy points at your trial. May even get off without serving jail time because of extenuating circumstances."

"I didn't have a choice!"

"We both know that isn't true. It may have been a terrible choice, but it was a choice all the same. You just made the wrong one."

CHAPTER 15

Thursday, 2130: Virginia Beach, Virginia

Julian is back," Tex said over the sounds of Kim's sobbing.

Elle hid her relief. "Good. Time for me to get to work." She walked over to Kim, who started freaking out more. "You're going to be gagged and blindfolded again. You can either cooperate and make this painless, or you can fight me, and I'll knock your ass out. And when you wake up, you'll be gagged and blindfolded anyway."

Kim stopped thrashing.

Elle put her gag and blindfold back in place and checked to ensure the cable ties on her wrists didn't have any signs of wear or weakness. The skin under them was raw to the point of bleeding. That would discourage any escape attempts, but Elle doubled the bonds just in case.

Elle jogged up the stairs to get her blood pumping a little. When she made the landing, she could see Julian emptying the contents of several canvas bags onto the living room floor. Before joining him, she checked in with Eve and Jack and gave them their new orders.

"We're going to send our email package at 0530 tomorrow and launch our message on all the screens starting at 0600. Between now and then, I need you guys to get creative and do whatever you can to find Anne Daniels. Start with her last known location. We have a small window of time when they could have moved her. It's not much, but I've seen you guys work miracles before," Elle said.

"Jack is already in the traffic camera system, so we may luck out by cross-referencing any vehicle departing the area during that window with DMV records. It's a long shot but worth a try," Eve said.

"If they left any kind of trail, we'll find them, Elle," Jack said.

"I know you will. Pace yourselves. You'll need to sleep and be ready to leave after we kick the hornet's nest in the morning and head back to the house in Woodbridge."

"Can I at least drive this time? I want to make it there before my next birthday."

Eve gave Jack a dirty look as her response.

Laughing, Elle said, "Go ahead and find yourself a car service or rideshare to take you back. Your choice. Just make sure it can't be connected to us." Moving to the living room, she peeked over Julian's shoulder and surveyed what he had brought back. He'd gotten everything she had asked for and then some. Several laser pointers and bungee cords completed the pile. "Well done. Any issues?"

"None. The old guy working there didn't even bat an eye when I put all this on the counter. A couple of kids came in and bought candy, but otherwise, I was the only customer. Didn't see any indications I had an audience."

"Let's hope our luck holds out a while longer. How do you feel about arts and crafts?"

"Babysitting, shopping, now arts and crafts time—the jokes almost write themselves. What am I making?"

"An IED."

"You have my attention."

"They'll be decoys and will never stand up to scrutiny, but they don't have to. Tom will have all his people on heightened alert. Even if they think they're fake, they won't risk taking a chance. It will provoke a reaction. And that's what we want. Use the putty, frosting, plastic wrap, and wiring to make something that looks like explosives."

"C4?"

"Or HME. One way or the other, it just needs to pull their focus, even for just a few seconds. We can use the putty for shape and the frosting for coloring. Wrapped in plastic and wiring with a timer in the center, should at a minimum make them cautious."

"How many do you want?"

"As many as we have material for. While you're starting that, I'll sketch out our game plan. Hand me the notebook and pencils."

Elle used the second tablet to pull up the overhead imagery of the airfield as a reference. Drawing the facility, she added the details they discovered during their reconnaissance. There was water on three sides of the place.

An inlet to the north, the bay to the west, and another one to the south. Only the eastern side had a proper land entry. Good thing she had a SEAL backing her. She was going to need someone very comfortable in the water. As she studied the image, she started marking off points where she wanted to place her decoys.

Satisfied with the plan, she set the pad aside and helped Julian build the fake explosives. They were able to make six total decoys. It wasn't much, but it would have to do. Grabbing the duffel bags with their small armory, Elle laid out everything they had left. She hoped it would be enough. Selecting the best rifle, she consolidated all the ammunition she could for that AR-15. She set the other rifle to the side. Then Elle took the shotgun and her SIG, made sure they were fully loaded, and placed them back in a duffel bag. She'd attached her suppressor to the SIG—just in case.

"Other than my SIG, we have six pistols left. Tex will need one, and I'll take a backup. Leaving four ladies looking for a dance partner. What do you want?" Elle asked, gesturing to the remaining guns in front of them.

"I'll take two Glocks and whatever ammo I can."

They had enough ammunition left for each weapon to have one extra magazine. Elle jammed the chosen few and put what was left with the discarded rifle and remaining pistols. "At least you have four mags for the rifle, but only one extra for each of the Glocks. Going to need to make every shot count."

"I'll try. What's the plan?"

Laying the diagram she'd drawn out, Elle said, "It's going to be a multi-phase mission with two main parts.

Part one is the assault on the airfield and killing Tom Matthews. There's a neighborhood on the other side of both the north and south inlets. I want you to bring me into the southern point, and then you drive around to the northern location. Leave the SUV someplace that you can get to it quickly and that it's not going to draw the attention of the neighbors. We're going to cross the inlets and infiltrate through the wooded areas that border the airfield. Be on the lookout for any cameras, alarms, or booby traps. There's a limit to what Tom could do without creating a higher profile for himself, but we can't be too careful right now. They've cleared the brush closest to their new fence line, but there's still plenty of cover to use. We need to be invisible."

"Shouldn't be a problem."

"That's the easy phase. We're going to split the decoys and the laser pointers. And this is where things are going to start getting crazy. Any camera you see, use duct tape to hold the laser pointer on it. Doesn't have to be perfect. Hell, doesn't even have to stay in place long. It just needs to stir shit up. Space out placing your decoys along the fence moving west to east. It will be dangerous as all hell the closer you get to the front since that will have the heaviest security presence. But I need you to find a nest near the front gate with a view of the hangers. Dig in if you can and take out anyone that's armed. If they make you, get the hell out of there and return to the SUV. Link up with the guys at the safehouse in Woodbridge for part two: rescuing Anne Daniels."

"I'm not leaving you behind, Elle."

"There's no other way, Julian. We can't stay together and get this done, and if you get caught or killed trying to come for me.... No. It's not an option. You need to let me handle my role in this. I'm not a damsel in distress, and I don't need to be rescued by the handsome prince. No matter how charming he is."

"I'm not patronizing you, Elle. Leaving you on your own against something like this goes against every instinct I have. I'd never leave a team member behind."

"In this case, you have to. It's the mission, and it's no different than any other time you've inserted someone behind enemy lines."

"This is different."

"No, it's not. We lose everything if I can't count on you, Julian."

He looked pained.

She leaned forward and kissed him. "I'm putting my trust in you. I need you to do this. Please."

His whole body was tense. Elle could only guess what was going on inside his head.

He gave a single nod and gripped her hand tightly. "Please don't make me regret this."

"All this ends tomorrow. I promise. Life can return to normal for all of you."

"What if that's not what I want?"

Elle felt like she had been knocked off her feet and was scrambling for purchase. She wanted to tell him how much he mattered but the words wouldn't come. "We need to relieve Tex, so he can finish his prep. Can you take the first shift?"

There was a long pause, and Elle wasn't sure if he would let the subject go. Eventually, he nodded. She started to stand up, but his grip on her hand tightened, and he pulled her back to him. The kiss was passionate and tender all at once.

When he pulled away, he leaned his forehead against hers and said, "I'm not letting this go. But for now, I know we have work to do."

As he walked away, Elle fought back the tears. *Not the time.* Standing, she returned to the small bedroom she'd napped in earlier and forced herself to lie down. Tomorrow would be the fight of her life, and she couldn't afford to think about anything else. Calling on every trick she knew, Elle attempted to clear her mind, but her charged emotions were like having a steel band cinched around her chest. Finally, she gave up the fight and did what Wise had taught her during their therapy sessions—she allowed herself to feel…everything. The tears flowed almost instantly. Finally, she fell asleep.

***

Friday, 0800: Virginia Beach

"She's ready, Tex. Let's do this." Elle double-checked Kim's bonds. "Don't try and escape. I have no problem returning you to the Agency with a few broken bones to make sure you don't go anywhere but where we want."

They each took a side and, together, hoisted Kim Daniels to her feet. She was unstable but didn't try to resist or run. Elle opened the doors as Tex helped her to the Civic. They got Kim situated in the back and added another layer of security by binding her hands and feet together. They left just enough slack to secure her seat belt.

"I don't like not having constant eyes on her, but I don't think she's going anywhere. Or going to try anything. Just keep as low of a profile as you can between here and there. If for some reason you get made, leave her and escape. If you think you can call in Calloway for an assist, do it. One way or the other, stay safe and out of trouble."

"I've got this, Elle. Don't worry. But you better do the same. This bastard doesn't have a line he won't cross to take you out. He'd shoot up a pre-school just to wound you," Tex said.

"I'm counting on it."

"Say it, Elle. Swear to me that you're going to survive this."

She considered lying to him flat out but decided on a more measured response. "I swear that's my intent. That's the best I can give you."

"I suppose that's better than nothing." He walked around to the driver's side of the car and started to get in but stopped. "See you on the other side, Mama."

It was like a hammer strike to the chest. Elle was afraid to even breathe and risk breaking down in tears. All she could do was nod and watch Tex get in the car and back out of the garage.

I love you, too.

Using the walk up the stairs to compose herself, Elle checked in with Eve and Jack. "How's everything going so far, guys?"

"A few amateur trace attempts but nothing significant yet," Jack said.

"The emails were sent this morning as planned. But I haven't seen anything come from it. They must be trying to verify the source," Eve added.

"They probably have a team of lawyers all over this. And law enforcement. The news networks will hit the air about it as soon as they agree on how to present the story without facing a libel suit. Once the story breaks, the politicians we sent the files to will start releasing statements. Then all hell will break loose."

"We'll stay on it. What do you need from us now?" Eve asked.

"Get ready to move. The car service taking you back to the safehouse in Woodbridge will be here soon. Tex may beat you guys there, but we're all going to lay low there until the dust settles from tonight. Then, you guys should be able to get back to your lives."

"You guys? Don't you mean we?" Eve asked.

"Even without Tom in the picture, I'm still a burned spy, Eve. There are a lot of people who are going to want me dead now that they know who I am. I can't go back to the way things were. But I can take control of my life again. And that's what I'm doing."

Eve looked sad, but she smiled when she said, "You deserve to be in control. We're with you, Elle. Whatever's next for you, you don't have to go it alone."

Her team was killing her. Wise would be pissed at her for putting a stranglehold on her emotions, but she couldn't afford to break down now. "One thing at a time, Eve."

"Ha! Owned you punk!" Jack yelled.

Jerking around, Elle asked, "What happened, Jack?"

"We had someone try to trace the email package, but I flipped the switch on them. Sent their signal right back to them, Goldeneye-style. So instead of them finding us, I found them. It's coming from the Earth airfield. Tom's people are there trying to track us."

"Do they have any idea where we are?"

"You're kidding, right?"

"Just give me a straight answer, Jack. I can't afford to make any assumptions right now."

"No, Elle. If they try to follow the trail they *think* they found, it will take them to Pennsylvania. Figured I'd point them in that direction since that's where Daniels is from."

"Nice touch. Well done."

"The car is here," Julian announced.

"Could you vet the driver and then help them get their gear loaded?"

"No problem."

"Things are heating up. They've upped their game. I'm guessing I can keep control of the boards for maybe another twenty minutes or so. Any longer, and I can't guarantee we won't get traced."

Elle looked at her watch. It'd been several hours since they launched their attack against the congressman. "If Tom's people are trying to trace the email, it's getting the kind of attention we want. Eve, any breaking news yet?"

"Not that I've seen—Wait…yep, here we go. The headline is Congressman Daniels implicated in human trafficking scandal. Wow, I still haven't gotten used to how that sounds."

"And you shouldn't ever get used to it. Jack, unless things get more intense, hold onto the boards for ten more minutes and then cut our connection."

"Too easy," he said.

"Alright. It's time. Do you guys have any final questions?"

"It's pretty straightforward, Elle. We've got this," Jack said.

Eve got up and gave Elle a fierce hug.

"You already hugged me, Eve. Or did you forget?"

"I hugged Tex a couple of times before he left, too. Deal with it," Eve said.

She returned the hug and said, "Well, he is a delicate flower. Thank you for looking out for him, Eve." Elle gave her friend one last squeeze and then backed away before her control started slipping.

"Jack, double your efforts to stay off the grid. I need you to be extra cautious until this is over. Eve, please stay vigilant."

"I promise, Elle. We'll be careful. Just please, promise me you'll do the same."

Elle smiled. "It's just a little stroll in the park, kid. Besides, you guys have the hard part. But you're going to find Anne Daniels, I know it." Moving over to Jack, she ruffled his hair. "Don't get cocky, Jack. Even superheroes can get caught sometimes."

Jack swatted at her hand, but then his eyes met hers.

She squeezed his shoulder before walking away. Going to the bathroom, she locked the door and slid to the floor. The weight of her emotions was crushing, and she couldn't hold them at bay anymore.

After a minute, she stood and splashed cold water on her face. *Time to finish this.*

Leaving the bathroom, she changed her clothes to gray yoga pants and a black long-sleeved moisture-wicking shirt. It wasn't her usual raid attire, but it would have to do. Packing the gear she wasn't taking with her, she dropped the bag in the living room for Julian to load into the car service with Eve and Jack. Then she tried on the new water shoes. They fit well enough that she didn't think blisters would be an issue. Regardless, she was going to have to make them work.

She preferred jeans and tennis shoes to what she was wearing, but with a water entry, the less waterlogged she was, the better. Using a trash bag and duct tape, she sealed up the weapons and gear to keep it watertight. She was doing the same for Julian's pack when he walked back into the room, wearing water shoes and shorts.

"Shorts? You know how cold the water is going to be this time of year, right?"

"Compared to Coronado in the winter, this is going to be like a hot spring."

"What made you buy that get-up?"

"You asking me to pick up water shoes for a raid. Figured I should be ready to back you up," Julian said.

She didn't even try to hide her smile. "Were you a boy scout in a previous life?"

"Thought about it but wasn't big on selling popcorn."

"Eve and Jack?"

"On their way to Woodbridge. No issues."

"We have a few hours before we need to leave. We should do final gear checks and get some rest."

"We should. And we will. But since we have the time..." Julian crowded in close, and Elle felt her body react in direct contrast to her brain.

"The last thing either of us needs is to talk about anything other than the mission," Elle said.

"Who said anything about talking? I think you already know everything I want to say."

Training warred with desire, but not for long. They would never have another moment like this, and Elle didn't want to let it pass. Closing the distance between them, Elle blocked out everything but Julian.

CHAPTER 16

Friday, 1900: Virginia Beach, Virginia

Ready? It's time for us to start pulling our weight around here," Elle said.

Julian snagged their bags and said, "Ladies first."

Tossing the bags in the cargo area, they jumped into the SUV. Backing out of the garage, Elle tensed. She scrutinized everywhere. Looking for anything that could mean danger. As long as their position hadn't been compromised, they were safer here than anywhere else. But that fact didn't ease Elle's anxiety.

The broken radio in the SUV didn't help matters either. *No music—damnit.*

They didn't speak the entire trip north. Elle was grateful for that. Julian always seemed to intuit what she needed. Periodically, he would reach over and take her hand. Much to her surprise, she didn't hate it. It was such a simple gesture, but it helped ground her to the moment.

She felt connected to him, and for some reason, that calmed her.

The sun was setting, and it would be dark soon. Traffic was heavy but flowing. Julian turned off the highway just south of Arlington on the Eastern Shore. He started weaving through the neighborhood where Elle would be dropped off. It was beautiful and had to cost a fortune. The houses were angled to capitalize on their waterfront location. Combined with the privacy afforded by the trees, it was a peaceful slice of paradise. It made it easy for them to drive straight through the neighborhood without drawing anyone's eye.

When they got to the end of the road, Julian pulled off to the side using the trees as a screen. Once the car was in park, he turned to her and said, "We could just keep driving."

"Tempting. Raincheck?" Elle said as she started getting ready to go.

"Going to hold you to that."

The tone of his voice made her pause. "Julian, I need your word that no matter what happens, you won't come inside that fence tonight. Stick to the plan. I'm going to have to do a lot of improvisation once I'm in there, and I can't afford to worry about friendlies in the mix. If I can treat everyone inside as hostile, I have a lot more options. And a higher chance of success."

"Only if you give me your word that you're coming back."

"You know as well as I do—that may be beyond my control. If you just want to hear the words anyway, then I promise, I'll come back. But one thing I can say with confidence is that I won't quit."

"I know. This is who you are. And I love you, anyway."

It was like all the air got sucked out of the car. "Julian—"

"Don't, Elle. Yes, I mean it. Yes, I know you—better than you know yourself. No, I don't expect you to feel the same. But I'll be damned if we go into something like this without letting you know how I feel. And when we get clear of this, I'm still going to mean it."

He got out of the SUV and walked around to her side. Opening the door, he held out his hand. She took it and was momentarily distracted by the way her legs shook. Julian pulled her into his arms and held her tightly before leaning in and kissing her.

Elle wasn't sure how long they stood there, but, eventually, he pulled away. Julian grabbed her duffel out of the SUV and handed it to her. Her hands stopped trembling as soon as she gripped the bag. *Game on.*

"Ready for this?" she asked him.

"Yes, ma'am."

"Then let's move."

Julian nodded. As he moved back around toward the driver's side of the SUV, Elle pulled the floor mat out from the passenger side and shoved it in the duffle. "I'll see you soon," she said, closing the car door.

"I'm counting on it." He looked at her for a beat, and hopped in.

Elle watched him pull away, then turned and ducked into the trees. She would have been at the inlet in a few minutes if not for the damn trees. The canopy was thick enough that it was almost pitch black as she maneuvered through using the busted NVGs she'd taken after escaping the ambush at her house. But the foliage was also a blessing in disguise. There was no way anyone would be able to monitor for movement here. She was essentially invisible. The second she made it to the inlet, that all changed. It was a wide crossing with no concealment. She was at a disadvantage. If the jet skis they saw earlier were patrolling, she was screwed.

The shadows went from black to gray between the trunks. She was close. Elle edged her way to the final tree between her and the water, then stopped. There was plenty of illumination tonight, and it looked like she was about to walk onto a dancefloor through the NVGs. This crossing was larger and riskier than the one she'd assigned to Julian but, with the extra drive to his start point, if everything played out correctly, they would both be in position at the same time. Seconds were flying by. She needed to move, but instinct held her in place. Something wasn't right.

Keeping to the shadows, Elle searched the area in front of her. Nothing jumped out. Was she imagining things? Indecision warred in her head—go or wait longer? She was about to step forward when a sound caught her attention. Something bumped against a rock, making a hollow sound. Moving around the tree, she leaned out to get a clear view of the bend in the shoreline. She could just make out the outline of the heads of two people behind a rocky outcropping. From the way they swayed, they were out on the water, probably sitting on the damn jet skis.

Well, at least she knew where they were now. This was going to change her plans dramatically. Going around wasn't an option. The terrain would be treacherous and take way too long, and she couldn't leave enemies at her back. The question now: How was she going to take them out? A gunfight would give away her position and alert the local police. Drawing them into the forest wasn't going to work. The sentries would be idiots to come chasing after her. Even if she managed to get them to follow, they would report the activity.

Time to go bold. Digging into the duffel, she pulled out her SIG with the suppressor. Studying their movement, the distance, and the visibility—she didn't like her odds. Elle had to make sure she took them out in rapid succession. Two shots, two kills, no other options.

Leaving the duffel, she crept through the trees at a snail's pace. She fought to maintain silence, pouring her focus into being invisible.

Though she didn't hear any noise, Elle was within twenty yards, close enough to see a soft glow of light, and both men tense. *Cell phone? Is that how the sentries are communicating?* With the cell jammer in place, they must be using Wi-Fi connectivity. Then one engine fired up.

Time's up.

Elle opened fire on her targets, one right after the other as she ran forward. The soft sand grabbed at her feet, slowing her efforts, but she persisted. They couldn't escape. The shadow closest to her toppled over, but the second seemed to waver a moment before disappearing from view. Elle closed the distance, stopping on the far side of the rocks. She didn't hear anything.

They were dead or waiting in ambush.

All her options sucked. Whatever angle she took, she risked getting her head blown off the second they saw her. Snatching a loose rock from the outcropping, Elle tossed it over the top to where her targets had been. A yelp told her someone was still alive and that she had landed one hell of a lucky shot. She lunged forward and sighted in on the movement. There was someone upright in the water. Squeezing off two more rounds, she pulled back and waited again.

Nothing.

She braced for a counterattack as she quartered her way around the rocks. Two forms floated in the water and were beginning to get pulled away by the current. Elle advanced on them, not trusting this wasn't a trick, ready to fire at the first twitch. The rocks were uneven but manageable. The closer she got, the more precarious her position became. If they were still alive, she had nowhere to go but straight at them.

A leg moved—Elle fired at both figures without hesitation. No reaction. Had that been real or just nerve twitches? Even after death, muscles could still contract. A slight glow caught her eye under the surface of the water near the bodies, about three feet down, she determined. Jumping into the water, she reached in and grabbed the cell phone. Pulling it up, she could just see the message on the screen before it went dark.

She's here.

They were coming for her.

No point in being subtle. Grabbing the jet ski that was already running, Elle maneuvered around the outcropping to the general area where she'd left her duffel. Dismounting as soon as the bottom touched the sand, she ran up to the tree line and began a rapid search. It didn't take long. Recovering the bag, she pushed the jet ski out and hopped on. Elle flew across the inlet and angled out to the bay. She wanted to approach the airfield from the back—a waterside attack to pull the guards away from the front and give Julian more of a chance to get in position ahead of them.

Nearing the jetty outside the airfield, Elle saw that spotlights now flooded the fence line. *Come and get me.* She pushed the jet ski past the waterline and, going full force, rode it as far up the bank as it would go. Then, leaping off, she ran for the closest camera. Grabbing one of the decoys and a laser pointer, she brandished the fake IED at the camera and gave them the finger. Then she turned on the laser pointer and aimed it at the camera. The laser would obscure any footage and could burn out the camera over time.

Moving to the closest tree, she pulled out the duct tape and attached the laser pointer to a branch. It was rudimentary and would never last, but she just needed to buy a few minutes. With the laser secure, she ran to the fence and pulled out the floor mat she'd removed from the SUV. Shouldering the duffel, Elle climbed as fast as she could while holding the floor mat. At the top, she looped the floor mat over the razor wire and used it as a path to clear the fence without serious injury.

The second she hit the ground, she was moving, sprinting toward the shadows in the center of the airfield and the hangars on the northern side. There was nothing for concealment. The only thing she had on her side was her brazen entry. She had moments before Tom took control of his guards and vectored them away from her decoy. He would know she was coming for him.

She was counting on it.

Headlights were approaching from the east.

Shit.

Grabbing her pistol and the second laser pointer out of the duffel, she kept running. She had seconds before they would be right on top of her—she had to make each one count. The SUV had been angling south, but then it changed course. They had her.

Elle stood her ground. Running wasn't going to do anything but wear her out until they shot her in the back. Removing the suppressor and NVGs, she hoped they wouldn't open fire before they were within range of her pistol. Movement on the passenger side of the SUV dashed those hopes.

Flipping on the laser pointer, she flashed it in the shooter's face before moving the beam to where the driver's head should be. Resting one wrist on top of the other, she held it in place, hoping to disorient the driver while aiming at the shooter. This would be a one-in-a-million shot. She squeezed the trigger and knew she missed but kept shooting. At least it was cover fire. Now, if she could just get the driver to veer away....

The echo of rifle shots startled her. The SUV swerved as a second shot followed right behind the first. The sudden erratic movement told her the driver had been hit. *Julian.* She simultaneously thanked and cursed him as she sprinted toward the vehicle. He'd once again saved her, but now he'd given away his presence. They'd be looking for him.

A shot of adrenaline coursed through Elle. The vehicle was still moving but at a much slower pace. It was coasting to a stop and didn't seem to be under anyone's control. Ready for a fight, she approached the passenger side and saw a slumped body. On full alert for an attack, Elle jumped on the running board and looked inside. The passenger was missing the back of his head, and the driver was choking on his own blood.

Elle put the driver out of his misery, then pulled open the passenger door. She threw the duffel in, then dove over the first body and onto the center console. She took a moment to clear the back seats. Nothing. Turning to the driver, she opened his door and pushed the body out using both legs with her back braced against the passenger seat. It toppled out with a thud, but the legs remained twisted in the door, one foot caught under the pedals. Sliding into the driver's seat, Elle whipped the vehicle around and gunned the engine. The body tumbled the rest of the way out, and the door swung shut. Driving back across the airfield, Elle searched the buildings for activity.

She could see more vehicles approaching, coming from the same location. It was the main terminal building. *Tom.* He'd want to be in the most fortified area and still be able to see. If he'd been smart, he would have bolted at the first alarm. But there was no way Tom would run from her, especially when he had home-field advantage and superior numbers.

The vehicles were coming straight at her, parallel to one another. This was one game of chicken that she intended to win. She reached over to the passenger side and picked up the orphaned AR-15. Flipping the selector to fire, she hooked the front grip over the side mirror for stability. She used her left hand to adjust the elevation and pull the trigger. Using the steering wheel to vector her bullets on target, she opened fire at the vehicle on her left. All she needed to do was land as many rounds as she could across the windshield. Didn't matter if they hit anyone. She just wanted the driver to maneuver away.

The headlights showed the windshield of the oncoming vehicle splintering but, instead of veering away, it accelerated forward. It was now a whole car length in front of the second, racing toward her at breakneck speed. Elle accelerated, too, and then swerved to the right seconds before they would have collided, emptying the rest of the magazine before dropping the rifle and gripping the wheel with both hands. She shot off the runway and into the grass, struggling to maintain control of the SUV with the sudden change in terrain.

Chancing a rollover, Elle made a quick left and heard an explosion of metal on metal before the back of the SUV jerked right. She felt the big vehicle lurch at an odd angle and steered into the movement to try and avoid wrecking. It felt like everything was moving in slow motion as Elle fought to get the SUV under control. When it happened, she almost couldn't believe she'd managed it. Stealing a look in the rearview mirror, she saw the wreckage of the other two SUVs. One of them must not have been able to anticipate the other, or her. Neither would be following her any time soon.

Her focus returned to the terminal building. She had been thrown widely off course, but now she circled around to aim the vehicle at the front door, where a small army was waiting. Pulling a couple of bungee cords out of the duffel, she tethered the steering wheel to the front seat and then threw the bag behind the passenger seat. She turned off the dome lights and hit the gas, setting the cruise control for twenty miles per hour. Jumping back to the center console, she opened the passenger door and kicked out the second body. This one didn't get tangled. Elle slid into the back, behind the driver's seat with one last glance to make sure they were still on course.

This is going to suck.

Bracing herself as much as she could on the floor, she waited for impact. Shouts and gunfire erupted everywhere around her, and then she was hurled forward and bounced into the air. She was thrashed around before slamming into the back of the driver's seat again. The duffel had landed on top of the seat, and she scrambled to grab it, ripping out a new pistol magazine. Doing a combat reload, she pocketed the half-spent magazine after seeding the full one into place. Keeping her head low, she peeked above the window line, taking advantage of the dark tint.

Five heavily armed men were advancing on the SUV.

Her ruse divided the security team. The rest of the men were on their way to check if she was the body they'd seen "jump" from the moving vehicle. The slow speed and low light had made it too probable for them to ignore. That still left a large group to deal with. The only cover available was several small offices along the far wall. She'd never make it there before they killed her.

Every muscle coiled in anticipation as she gripped the handle and leaned against the door. Pistol at the ready, she waited. A guard came close to the rear door. The windows were making them all cautious, and rightfully so. He shifted his weight and then released his non-firing hand to grab the door handle, the barrel of his weapon dropping as he moved to open the door so his partner could clear the inside. That's when Elle attacked.

Using the full force of her body weight, she propelled the door open. There was a satisfying cracking sound when it contacted the man's outstretched hand. The moment her barrel cleared the doorframe, she started firing. Not caring that they had body armor on, Elle fired at the first target she saw, knowing the impact at this range would be like a hammer blow to the chest—giving her a split second to make the kill shot. Two to the head, and then she was back on the guard by the door. His broken hand slowed him down just enough for her to come out victorious. But the fight wasn't over.

The guard standing by the tailgate, watching his team as they flanked her on both the sides of the vehicle, opened fire—full automatic.

Elle jumped back into the SUV, hitting the floor and covering her head. Everything around her exploded. Shards of glass and debris from bullets shredding plastic and upholstery rained down. Time stretched out into eternity as she waited for a round to find its way to her.

Then…silence.

"As much as I'm enjoying watching this, Elle. It's too much of a heroic end, and we both know that's not you. Besides, I'm not done with you yet."

The sound of triumph in Tom's voice made the floor just fall out from under her. She was trapped.

CHAPTER 17

Friday, 2130: Eastern Shore, Virginia

"Come out, Elle. Now. Or I'll have my men finish what they started. And your hands better be clearly visible—and empty," Tom said.

Her mind raced, desperately trying to find a way out. Sitting up cautiously, she saw Tom standing behind the three remaining guards. His dark hair and complexion made his toothy, smug smile stand out even more. His linen jacket looked a little boxy—he had to be wearing a Kevlar vest underneath. All the angles were covered. There were no options left but to comply. The gravity of her situation was crushing, and her legs shook as she started to move.

The burn of hatred steadied her. There would be an opportunity. She just needed to be ready for it. Kicking open the rear door on the driver's side, Elle got out as though she had just finished a joy ride. Dusting off all the particles on her clothes, she smiled at the men glaring back over their gun sights. "No hard feelings, guys. But stuff like this is going to happen when your boss is a narcissistic piece of shit."

"Hands, Elle. Keep them where we can see them. No sudden moves, or this is going to be over sooner than either of us want."

"Easy, Tom. You sound worried. Shouldn't you be boasting about your master plan like every other douchebag?"

"Who else is with you?"

Elle shrugged.

"No point in playing games. My men will handle your friends. Who jumped from the SUV? One of your pets? Agent Traviano or your new toy: Saunders?"

"I have everything I need to end this, thanks to you, Tom," Elle said.

Tom laughed. "I assume you're trying to imply that I have a traitor in my ranks. Create doubt. Breed mistrust. It's not going to work. I'll have my answer soon enough. I may even let you beg me for their lives."

Elle's emotions and thoughts churned. She scanned the faces of his men as an excuse to look around. If she could get past them, she could get outside and use the shadows to disappear. The only other option was to go farther into the building, but that meant turning her back on them.

"Where are the explosives?" Tom demanded.

"You'll find out soon enough."

"Nice try. They're either along the perimeter, on the airfield, or still in the SUV." Then, looking at the guard at the end, Tom said, "Search the vehicle."

The two remaining guards tensed as their companion moved away toward the SUV as if expecting her to react.

Instead, she winked—though she was about to lose her gear. And weapons. The air was getting heavier, and Elle was having a hard time keeping her hands from shaking.

"IED!" the guard called.

The tension ratcheted up even more, and the two remaining guards pushed Tom out of the hangar—all the while he was fighting it and glaring at her. "It's not real. Is it, Elle?"

"Sir, we'll need to clear it. Until then, the farther away you are, the better. Three hundred yards at a minimum would be best, but the jet in the hangar should give you enough cover to avoid serious injury."

Tom looked irritated, but his body language told Elle he was unsure about the level of danger. "Fine. Strap her to the vehicle. If it goes up, she goes up with it. Once you clear the device, bring her to me." Tom smirked before turning and walking away.

"C'mon, guys. Do you really want to do this? He orders you into the line of fire, gets your boys killed, and then just goes and rides out the fireworks on his fancy jet. No paycheck is worth that bullshit."

"Move your ass, bitch."

"Worth a try," Elle said as she sat on the tailgate of the SUV.

One of the guards threw a pair of flex-cuffs at her. "You know the drill."

Picking up the cuffs, she slipped her wrists through the loops and used her teeth to tighten them. "Now what?"

"Now, you're going to tell us what kind of device we're dealing with. We're going to find out, anyway, so don't waste our time." Turning to another guard, he ordered,

"Call Zach and Ben back from the perimeter search. This device is the priority."

The man nodded and was about to make the radio call when another voice came over the comms. "We made it to the vehicle jumper. It's Dan. She must have pushed him—"

The radio cut off just as a rifle shot rang out. It was followed by a second and a third and then a barrage of answering fire. Elle could see muzzle flashes from two guns, one low to the ground—an injured man, returning fire at an unseen threat. Julian, again.

"I've got her. Go, go!" her captor ordered.

The other two men ran out and took fire. Screaming caused her guard to look away for a fraction of a second—Elle took the opening. She'd cuffed her wrists together but not to the vehicle. She spun around and jumped into the SUV as bullets chased her. The duffel was wide open, exposing the fake IED. Elle snatched the remaining pistol from her bag and went on the offensive. Julian would be running out of ammunition fast, and more men were coming. They had his position and would be going for him. She needed to level the playing field.

The flex cuffs cut into her wrists and made her movements awkward. But it was kill or be killed. The guard was firing as he advanced. He wasn't interested in capturing her again. Orders be damned. Rolling from the vehicle on the far side, she risked being killed by the other guards, but they were focused on Julian. Shifting forward to put the engine block between her and her pursuer, Elle waited for a lull in his shots. He would either pause to conserve ammunition or run out.

It sounded like he was right behind her when the volley of shots abruptly stopped. Whipping around, she started firing in the direction of the last shot before chancing a look over the hood of the SUV. A round had hit home, causing her pursuer to pause in his reload. His new magazine forgotten—the barrel of the AR-15 dropped toward her—which meant there was still a round in the chamber. Throwing herself sideways, Elle repeatedly fired at the man's head before slamming into the ground. She hit at an awkward angle. Air rushed out of her lungs, and, as her head struck concrete, she saw a kaleidoscope of iridescent lights. But she managed to hold onto her gun.

Fighting to clear her vision, Elle tried to get to her feet, but her head swam, forcing her to stumble and fall back down. The ringing in her ears was pierced by the sound of the rifle shot, the tumble saving her life. The final round from her enemy's weapon snapped past her head by a fraction of an inch.

The dull click of an empty rifle is the loudest sound in a gunfight, and it put everything back into focus. Elle's equilibrium returned just as her adversary tried to transition to his sidearm. It was a race to the death, and the advantage was now hers. Rolling over on her back, she pulled the trigger, feeling the satisfying recoil of the pistol first and then a hollow clink. Her magazine must have become unseeded during her fall. Training took over, and she slammed the bottom of the magazine with her palm. With her hands bound, she struggled to rack another round into the chamber, using the crook in her leg behind her bent knee to grip the slide.

When the man's body dropped by her feet, Elle almost didn't believe it. Her first shot had found its mark. Sitting up, her head screamed, and her vision started to swim again. Less this time, but it was still alarming. She crawled over the body to put the SUV between her and the fighters outside. The exit wound in the back of his head negated the need to verify he was dead. Elle dug through his pockets and found a knife.

Slicing through the flex cuffs, she felt a trickling sensation run down her neck. Once her hands were free, she inspected the back of her head and winced at the contact. Her hand came away covered in blood. The last thing she needed right was to deal with a head wound, let alone blood loss.

For starters, there was no time.

Grabbing the AR-15, the radio, and the two remaining magazines, Elle stood, testing her limits. She was a little shaky but managed. She loaded the gun and used the cell phone pocket in her yoga pants to house the last magazine. *Guess these things are useful after all.* Checking around the SUV, she could no longer see the other shooters. The night had gone quiet. How many were left? Were they with Tom, or had they gone in pursuit of Julian?

One way to find out.

Edging around the vehicle, Elle grabbed the duffel and slung it over her shoulder. She reloaded with her last magazine and tucked the pistol in the outside pocket of the duffel with the radio. The shotgun was still inside, as were her tools and the fake IED. Holding the AR-15 at the ready, she jumped into the fray. Quartering the opening she'd created with the SUV, Elle saw a body on the ground. Checking as she started her run at the building, she counted several more. A few of Tom's men were still alive. But where?

Keeping to the shadows created by the buildings as much as possible, Elle made her way toward the hangar. Tom was the lynchpin. The fight would end with him. The expanse between the buildings was the only thing separating her and the hangar. No cover or concealment. If anyone was watching, there was no way to get past them without being spotted. It felt like an ambush.

Elle studied every inch of the roof of her target building. Whoever controlled the high ground had the advantage. She'd want eyes up there. Her muscles tensed as the all too familiar feeling of being watched overtook her. Reacting on instinct, she pulled back and ducked. Debris followed close behind as several large rounds tore through the side of the control building.

Staying low, Elle scrambled back into the control building. *Fucking .50 cal sniper rifle.* Just one of those rounds would turn her into pink mist. She needed a new plan. Using the SUV again wasn't going to happen. One glance told her it was out of commission.

She ran back into the terminal building and searched all the rooms until she found stairs leading to the air control tower. Keeping below the window line as she moved, she stopped to peek. She was almost even with the roof of the hangar. But she couldn't make out any details in the dark or open any of the windows. The shooter could be anywhere, and they were much better equipped for this kind of fight.

Moving around the room, she read all the panels and screens until she came to the main power controls. She cut the power, and the entire field plunged into blackness. The sniper would have night vision capability. But if she could wreck his vision, she might have a chance to get to the hangar. Or maybe there was another way?

Pulling the radio out of the duffel, Elle keyed the mic. "How's it feel to be hunted? By my count, there are four of you left. Maybe less by now if anyone's found my surprises. For those of you still alive, this is your chance. Tom Matthews is going to die tonight. One way or the other. You can find another paycheck if you're smart enough to know when to walk away."

A moment passed before another voice came over the air. "You must be getting desperate, Elle. My men aren't going to fall for your bullshit," Tom said.

"If you're so confident, Tom, why not have your men check in?"

"I know what you're doing. You're trying to get them to give away their positions. It won't work."

"Your men must have protocols for a situation like this. So, you can't really be concerned about them. Admit it—you're scared."

"I'm sick of your fucking mouth. Boys, kill her. Now."

Elle listened for any responses. Was she getting in their heads, or were they just using radio discipline? Hard to tell when she didn't know if any of them were there for more than the money. "I don't hear anyone acknowledging your orders, Tommy boy. Your platoon of mercenaries wasn't enough to stop me. How about you stop hiding in your cushy little toy plane and come face me yourself?"

No response.

Elle turned the radio off and put it back in the duffel. She didn't want them to be able to locate her by keying it up. Returning to the stairs in the dark, she pulled out the handgun and flashlight, then shouldered the bag and slung the rifle. Walking into the fatal funnel of the stairwell, Elle moved with stealth and care, by touch and memory, counting stairs as she descended while focusing her eyes on where her assailant would be. They had to have known where she was when the power shut off. At least one of them would be coming.

A faint, green glow came into her field of view. Without hesitation, Elle flipped on the flashlight and fired twice. The man barely had the chance to recoil from the searing pain of the bright light penetrating his NVGs before the bullets shattered one of the lenses and lodged in his skull.

As the body tumbled back down the stairs, Elle followed, hoping the corpse had a partner and the commotion tripped him up. The stairs were empty. Three guards left. Looking down at the man, she saw that he was slender and wearing all black tactical gear and a ball cap...

Through NVGs and with a bit of showmanship, it might work.

Removing the vest, pants, and ballcap, Elle dressed in his attire. Tucking her hair up in the ballcap, she tried not to dwell on how wet it was. Wiping her blood-covered hands on the dead man's shirt, Elle picked up the broken NVGs and rifle. His Molle vest had several additional magazines and a knife in a sheath. Digging the tools out of the duffel, she tucked them and the flashlight into an empty mag pouch.

The moon glowed through the gaping hole in the wall of the terminal she'd made with the SUV. Returning to the vehicle, she searched inside for an emergency roadside kit. There was one in the cargo area. Pulling it open, she found a single road flare. That would work. Staging one rifle near her planned exit, Elle got ready for her next firefight. Next, she staged the flare, a second rifle, and a shotgun on the hood of the SUV. She took a few seconds to practice switching between the weapons.

Grabbing the shotgun, she turned right and fired twice, smoothly switching weapons as she spun around and fired the AR-15 left. Transitioning again, she destroyed a window with the shotgun before grabbing the flare and igniting it. Then, she picked up the AR-15 and started running for the door as she tossed the flare in the pool of gas that had run out the back of the SUV. It lit up with a whoosh. Elle fired behind her as if she were being pursued and sprinted out of the building, angling for the hangar.

The ruse would buy her seconds at best, but that could be all she would need. The sniper would have heard the two different weapons firing and would be searching for the threat, assuming that his teammate was in a gunfight with their target. Her change in attire, demeanor, and being backlit by the fire would make it impossible to immediately identify that she was not a friendly.

Elle's muscles screamed in protest, but she pushed on. The open stretch between buildings felt like the fucking

Grand Canyon. Counting the seconds in her head, Elle angled her rifle upward and started firing at the roof ledge. She had to assume the sniper was close, set up to cover his compatriot. The closer to the hangar she got, the more they would have to lean out to get an angle on her—placing them in her line of fire.

Elle didn't slow the pace as the building neared, just tucked her head and shoulder and rammed into the door. It had been locked, but it was not set up to withstand a full assault. The frame splintered and gave way with a loud crack as Elle crashed through and landed on the concrete floor of the hangar. Sharp pain told something was broken. It hurt to breathe, and her head was spinning. But she was alive.

For now.

Struggling to get her bearing, Elle looked around. Emergency lights were on inside the hangar, casting an eerie red glow over everything. She could smell jet fuel and oil. There was a sleek-looking jet parked in the middle of the room. The door was open, and light was spilling out. An invitation.

A trap.

Elle pushed herself to her feet. Everything hurt, but her instincts, shrieking a warning, shot adrenaline through her body. Looking for cover, Elle moved to a stack of crates that appeared to be spare parts and froze. In the corner by the door, she saw a digital clock start to count down from ten minutes. Around the hangar, she could see other timers connected to windows and the rear door. The place was booby-trapped, and she activated the countdown when she breached the perimeter.

Fuck.

Tom would be the one with the code, and he would never shut it off unless she was already dead. So, she either had to retreat and allow the bastard to escape or find some way to kill him and get out of the kill zone in…nine minutes and thirteen seconds.

CHAPTER 18

Friday, 2150: Eastern Shore, Virginia

"Tick-tock," Tom's voice boomed over a loudspeaker.

There was no way he was on that plane. He was baiting her. Worse, she couldn't be sure that the sniper on the roof or one of the other remaining guards wouldn't be closing in, as well. The crack of a sniper rifle startled her. The shooter on the roof was still there—on the offensive. That could only mean one thing: Julian. Was he inside the fence line?

There was no way to warn him about the explosives. She had to kill Tom fast and find a way to warn Julian to retreat. All in less than nine minutes. Recalling what little she saw before hitting the cement floor, she asked herself: If she had been lying in wait—their roles reversed—where would she be?

Mobile.

The second the thought struck, she launched into action. Hoisting the rifle over her head, she fired blindly into the hangar, moving right to left. Wood crates creaking on her left gave away the location of her target. Jumping to her feet, Elle sprinted toward the crates, while using suppressing fire to close the distance. She caught the motion of a gun barrel clearing the side of a container and threw herself out of the line of fire. She hit the floor rolling, jolting to a stop as she slammed into the stack of crates that were shielding her enemy.

The 50 .cal on the roof cracked off again, followed by Tom's twisted laughter. "It seems like we've come to the end of our little game, Elle. You can't kill me. I'm the only thing keeping you alive."

What the hell is that supposed to mean? The bombs? Her mind kicked into overdrive. Something was wrong. "Is this the part where you brag about your plans for world domination?" Elle asked, stalling for time. Any move she made right now had about a 50/50 chance of success—on an even playing field. But the sinking feeling in her gut told her Tom was holding a winning hand.

"Trust me, you're going to want to see this with your own eyes."

"If I see a weapon, you're a dead man. No matter what kind of trick you've got up your sleeve."

"I don't need a weapon."

Stepping out from around the crates, he was just a few feet away. Elle almost shot him on reflex, but her eyes went to his hand, and she froze.

"Checkmate, bitch."

A dead-man switch. If Tom dropped it, the explosives would ignite regardless of the timers.

Elle rose to her feet, keeping the AR-15 leveled at her target. "So, what's your play? Murder-suicide?"

"I always have a backup plan, Elle. You, of all people, should know that. No matter what—I win. The only option you have is to run. Since it sounds like you have backup with you, you may even escape before they die, too."

"You're just going to let me walk away?"

"Run, actually. Think you can get out of the line of fire before I cue my sniper? Or get to my gun?"

Glancing over at the timer in the corner, she could just make out the numbers: 7:47 and counting. Should she wait it out? Would he hold this fucked up standoff until they both ran out of time? Did he want her dead more than he wanted to live?

Elle knew what her answer would be.

Shifting her weight and turning her eyes to the door, Elle gave the appearance of considering her escape options. Then, without a hint, she lunged, using the rifle as an extension of her arm, slamming the end of the barrel into his chest. The impact was jarring. It distracted him enough for Elle to grab his left hand with both of hers. Then she coiled his arm around her, much like a dance move. With her back against his chest, fighting the pain of her head wound, Elle slammed her head into his nose. Bright lights flashed across her vision, and she had to rely on touch to keep the fight going.

Stepping away, she raised his trapped hand and spun under his arm, wrenching it backward while striking at his knee with the heel of her foot. He checked the kick and went for the pistol tucked in the small of his back. He pulled the trigger with it still in the holster. The bullet ripped through the holster and his clothes before shredding the outside of her thigh.

Now!

Elle released a hand from the dead-man switch to pull the knife from her tactical vest. In one fluid motion, she ran it across Tom's neck. Blood sprayed, and she felt him go rigid as his right arm swung forward, gun in hand, in one last effort to kill her. Swinging the knife down against the inside of Tom's wrist, she sliced his tendons. The gun went clattering to the floor as its owner stumbled and fell.

Elle fought to keep control of the dead-man switch as they hit the ground. She lay across his body, using her weight to keep him pinned as he bled to death. His strength was fading, and, within seconds, she was able to wrestle his hand open. Once she had control of the switch, she stood gingerly. Everything hurt.

It was over.

She looked at Tom. A fresh gush of blood pushed out of his neck, releasing a gurgling sound. He choked out the words, "I win," then lost consciousness. The feeling of being in a trap was overwhelming.

Grabbing the neck of his shirt, she slashed it down the middle with her knife. Tom wasn't wearing Kevlar. It was a suicide vest. There were small, medical lead wires adhered to his pulse points and a heart monitor in the center of what looked like a block of C-4. Elle was on her feet and sprinting toward the closest window. The trigger for the vest had to be Tom's heart—she'd spent enough time hooked up to a heart monitor to know what she was seeing. And how they worked. Instead of an alarm, once he flatlined, it would blow. She had a few heartbeats at most.

Elle propelled herself, full speed, through the window, curling into a ball to protect her head and torso. Glass clawed at her arms and legs, shredding her skin. Her forearms ached from taking the brunt of the impact.

Keep going. Push harder.

Ignoring the pain, Elle braced for the fall, then willed her muscles to move, praying the sniper hadn't spotted her. She needed distance and something solid between her and the hangar. There was a second hangar, a few modular buildings, and one smaller, brick building. Angling toward the brick structure, she took off. She had no intention of stopping once she made it there, but she needed a shield between her and the shock wave and shrapnel the hangar would send flying in every direction.

She nearly made it when the explosion rang in her ears and the shock wave lifted her off the ground and sent her hurtling.

Then everything went black.

***

As Julian opened his eyes, he felt the oblivion of unconsciousness break and a wash of pain travel through him. Everything hurt, and he couldn't hear anything over the high-pitched tone shrieking in his ears from the explosion. He tasted blood, and his vision had a weird hallow effect. Lifting his head, Julian looked around. He was lying on the ground a few feet from the airfield gate. Using the fence for leverage, he hoisted himself up. As his mind cleared and his vision focused, he saw the inferno and realized what had happened. What was left of the hangar was burning. He could smell jet fuel, which explained the massive blaze. No longer concerned about the sniper, Julian started to run toward it, but a secondary explosion stopped him in his tracks. It was a small blast, but it told him all he needed to know about how unstable the scene was. No one was getting near the site any time soon.

Elle?

He'd watched her run into the hangar through his scope. Though disguised, he recognized her movements and thought, *That's one hell of a gamble with a sniper on the lookout.* When she started firing at the roofline, he'd done what he could to assist. He'd been too far and at a terrible angle to do any real damage—but a couple of well-placed rounds had pulled the shooter's attention away from her, and she'd made it inside.

Julian had kept the sniper's focus on him, almost enjoying the cat and mouse game. He'd been forced to come inside the fence when his opponent seemed to reprioritize his efforts. As far as he could tell, the asshole on the roof was the last mercenary standing, and he wasn't about to let him go after Elle. Then everything went to hell.

The wail of sirens registered over the ringing in his ears. Julian had to get out of there. He'd made a promise, and he wanted to keep it. But he felt terrible. Julian had never left a teammate behind, and Elle was so much more. Impulse said to run into the fray and search for her. What if she was injured and needed help? But he also had a teenage girl to rescue, which he'd been ordered to prioritize.

Julian started to run, but the first few strides were awkward. He felt uncoordinated and dizzy with the motion. Slowing his pace to try and regain his composure, Julian pressed on, as he did not want to run into law enforcement. Even if they were on the same side, he would have a lot of explaining to do if he was caught fleeing the scene. The list of felonies they could charge him with was extensive.

It took a minute to realize he couldn't make out the sound of the approaching sirens anymore. The roar of the massive blaze at the airport, periodic secondary explosions and the ringing in his ears made it hard to distinguish among the various noises. Looking back through the trees, he caught flashes of blue. The police either had incredible response times, or he'd been unconscious longer than he'd realized and left just in time. Picking up his pace, Julian pushed his limits to make up lost time.

By the time he made it to the inlet, his legs seemed to be functioning correctly again, but the increased blood flow aggravated the throbbing in his head. Stopping just before exiting the tree line, Julian took several deep breaths, cataloging how his body felt as his eyes searched for threats. Everything was quiet.

Entering the cold water, pain flared in several places on his upper body. He didn't have to look to know there would be fresh cuts there. Ignoring the burning sensation as he glided through the water, he hoped nothing had lodged inside them, and he wouldn't need stitches. He hated stitches.

Swimming had always been one of Julian's strengths, and he was across the inlet in no time. Nothing stirred in the darkness, and he was under the cover of the trees in seconds. Rushing back toward the SUV, he couldn't help but hope that it was gone. Not having a ride would make things challenging, but it would mean Elle was okay.

Julian emerged from the wooded section at the end of a residential area, slowing his pace to a stroll. The SUV looked empty and, just as he'd left it—parked along the cul-de-sac behind a group of other vehicles. There were several people outside their homes, so he angled his approach, making it look like he had come from the direction of the beach and not the woods. If any of them noticed him, they didn't give any kind of indication. There was no way they didn't hear the explosions. Had they already chalked it up to a terrorist attack? The first responders would have called for backup the minute they saw the blaze. Every three-letter agency in the book would be all over this area soon.

Making it to the SUV without being questioned, Julian slid behind the wheel and pulled away. He waved in acknowledgment at the neighbors that looked his way. They politely returned the gesture, as neighborly folks do.

It took a lot of self-control to obey the traffic laws and keep a low profile all the way back to the house in Woodbridge. His thoughts kept bouncing back and forth between Elle and the mission. Julian knew he needed to get into the right headspace. There was a young girl's life on the line. The only hope she had to make it through the night was to stick to the plan Elle had set into motion. Still, focusing was proving to be challenging.

Julian hit the steering wheel in frustration and fell back on his training to cope with the dilemma. As he drove, he assessed his injuries and took stock of his assets. The cuts on his extremities were shallow and, other than a headache and bruises, he seemed to be okay. The ringing in his ears and the pressure in his head had eased a little, but he probably had a slight concussion. He didn't have time to go through the standard aftercare for traumatic brain injury, but he'd seen the fallout from untreated TBIs enough times to know he needed to take it seriously. As soon as they had the girl, he would go to medical.

As for assets, he had the SUV. If Tex didn't find a way to get Director Calloway to help—they'd be in a world of hurt. And that was assuming that Calloway didn't detain Tex for what they'd already done. For all he knew, they might all be wanted right now, and he was a fugitive with nothing but his bare hands and his wits to keep him alive.

He'd take those odds.

Satisfied with that assessment, he turned his attention to the road and his breath. The best thing he could do right now was keep his blood pressure down. That would help ease the effects of the concussion.

There weren't any direct routes back to Woodbridge off the peninsula of the Eastern Shore. Julian was forced to take the northern one to avoid going back toward the airfield. He didn't want to chance crossing paths with any cops if he could help it. That made the trip take over four hours. But the lack of traffic made the drive smooth and easy and helped ensure no one was following him.

By the time he got back to the house, the headache had dulled, and the ringing was less noticeable. He parked the SUV two blocks away and walked. His muscles were tight, and his body protested, but the movement helped him work out the kinks. Approaching the house on high alert, he didn't see anything amiss, so he knocked on the door.

He heard two sets of footsteps and then sensed he was being looked at through the peephole. Then the door was opened, and he was assailed by a flurry of questions.

"Oh, thank god, Julian. Are you okay? You look hurt. Do you need anything?" Eve asked. She refrained from hugging him as she eyed the bloodstains all over his clothes.

Tex smiled and stepped back to allow him entry and closed the door.

But Julian could tell something was wrong. "Elle isn't here, is she?"

Tex hesitated. "You're the first one back. We were hoping you would come back together. Do you have any idea where she is? Or what happened?"

"I honestly don't know. I'll fill you in on everything later, but we're out of time. I have every reason to believe that Tom Matthews is dead—which means the clock is ticking on the Anne Daniels rescue."

Jack's voice broke in from the other room, "I've got it!"

Tex put a hand on Julian's shoulder. "Perfect timing, Jack!" Then, looking at Eve and Julian, he said, "Let's get to it."

CHAPTER 19

Saturday, 0230: Woodbridge, Virginia

"They're selling Anne," Jack said.

"When?" Tex asked.

"Now. On the dark web. I was able to track the seller, but that's not where the girls are."

"Girls?" Eve asked.

"Anne isn't the only girl being sold. There are at least twenty being auctioned off to the highest bidder," Jack said.

"What makes you think the girls aren't with the seller?" Julian asked.

"Because I bought one of them," he said.

"You did what!?!" Eve shrieked.

"It was the only way I could think of to get the information we need. Once I was a paying customer, contact was established. That was all I needed to get inside their system. They're giving all the buyers the same location with different delivery instructions. The girls have to be there," Jack answered.

"Where the hell did you get the funds?" Tex asked.

"Didn't need money, just access. They just think they got paid. Won't stand up to any scrutiny, but I was counting on you guys doing the hero thing before they find out I cheated them."

"Happy to oblige," Tex said. "How much time do we have?"

"I'm not sure. The sales have delivery times that are pending completion of the auction. And there's a bidding war going on…for Anne. It looks like they're using the media storm around her uncle to drive the price up."

"I don't understand. Why would the buyers risk going after someone so high profile?" Eve asked.

"The risk is part of the thrill. It's not just about sex. It's about power. Some of these pervs will want to leverage Anne like Tom did," Jack said. "But this is a good thing for us. Buys us time to get her out. They're less likely to kill her when she's pulling in that much interest."

"So, where are we going?"

"Back to D.C., to a private storage company near Dulles. It's owned by the same shell corporation as Earth Airport. Eve, can you take it from here? Someone is trying to track me."

Eve looked over Jack's shoulder and then jumped on her laptop. After a few moments, she turned the computer around to display an overhead image of the location. It looked like every other storage unit facility out there. "There's one entrance and one exit. It's a large facility, but most of it is just single-story compartments."

"Do we have any support?" Julian asked.

"Yeah, but there's a hitch," Tex said. "Eve and Jack have been busy. They found our targets but, in the process, discovered that every time law enforcement gets close to these guys, they clean house and bolt. Their victims are disposable to them. We can't risk them killing those girls. Calloway will send in the cavalry, but we stand a better chance of keeping people alive if it's just us."

"I agree. What have we got to work with?" Julian asked.

Tex led him out of the living room and into the dining area.

Two large, black duffel bags along with several weapons cases lay on the table. Inside each bag was a full tactical loadout, including body armor, ammunition, comms gear, and clothes. "Looks like Christmas came early this year," Julian said.

"And no one believed me when I told them I was on the nice list," Tex said as he dug through the other bag. Then, tossing a first aid kit to Julian, he added, "Go get yourself cleaned up. I'll get all the mags jammed, and we can talk strategy when you're not bleeding all over the place."

"It's just a couple of scratches, so it should only take a few minutes. Try not to have too much fun without me." Julian grabbed the clothes out of his bag and left.

"No promises."

Julian jogged up the stairs and forced himself to stay on task. Closing the bathroom door, he stripped and started the shower. Someone, probably Eve, had placed towels and travel-sized toiletries on the counter. Grabbing some soap, he paused when he saw his reflection in the mirror. Damn, no wonder Eve had looked so concerned. Blood was everywhere. Most of it was tacky now, but there were still wet spots. He'd need to clean the wounds to determine the extent of the damage.

Letting the water irrigate his wounds, Julian cleaned off all the blood that had oozed out and crusted over during his lengthy car trip. He'd been lucky that his egress route took him for a swim before any civilians saw him, or he'd have tripped every alarm, even in the dark. As it was, he just looked wet—not bloody.

Several of the cuts on his arms had debris embedded under the surface, and he found a small puncture on his right side. It took some scrubbing with gritted teeth to get that wound clean, but he managed. Luckily, the Navy had taken every chance they got to stab him with needles. So, he was relatively certain he was up to date on his tetanus…and all the other preventative measures. He'd still need the pros to check him out when all this was over to avoid secondary effects. But, for now, a quick patch job would have to do.

Slathering on antibiotic ointment, he paid particular attention to the areas that were still bleeding. Bandaging the worst offenders, he stood for a minute, looking in the mirror to see if he missed anything. He looked like he'd been through a warzone, which wasn't far off, but he'd avoided serious injury. Dressing, he pulled on the black tactical gear he'd been given. Impressive stuff. The material was sturdy but light, with lots of give for range of motion. After he tugged on the Salomon boots, he was ready to go.

Jogging back down the stairs, he rejoined Tex in the dining room. All the magazines were lined up on the table. Tex was in the middle of a function check on an M4 carbine. "You look better, but that's not saying much. Are you good?"

"I'm good. You think this is bad? You should have seen me after Hell Week," Julian responded.

"The bidding war is slowing down, Tex," Jack called. "They'll start moving the girls as soon as all the sales are made. You and Julian need to get on it."

"You ready?" Eve asked.

Tex grabbed the tablet with the overhead view of the location. "It's a business area, so it's going to be pretty empty. We've got about two hours before sunrise. We need to get in, find the girls, and take out the guards before they know we're there."

Zooming out, Julian studied the surroundings. They could try and walk in, but most businesses had security cameras. How would they know if they were compromised? Elle would kill him if she knew what he was about to propose. "We're going to need some help on this one."

"What do you have in mind?" Tex asked.

"Eve. Have her in a vehicle across the street from the location—with the overhead lights on, checking her hair and makeup. She draws it out so that anyone watching knows that there's a beautiful woman, alone, in a car. She can keep checking her phone, too, like she's supposed to meet someone," Julian said.

"A beautiful woman and an illicit rendezvous. If I were a hired lackey, that would definitely hold my attention more than guard duty. But these guys are supposed to be pros. They'll be suspicious."

"We can still use it. Even if they think it's a lure, it'll force them to divide their focus, creating a window for us."

"The east side is the most vulnerable, so they'll make sure that's covered. The north looks like it's too open. They'd see us coming, so that leaves us to approach from the west. We can use this alley to get close, but if they don't have cameras set up to cover that area—they're idiots. We'd be exposed trying to climb over the storage units, and I doubt we'll find much there to get a handhold. We'll need a boost…or a grappling hook. Know any ninjas?"

"Isn't that part of Ranger training?" Julian asked.

"Remind me again why I like you?" Tex asked.

Smiling, Julian said, "I think we hit two sides simultaneously. East and west. You're right—they'll send bodies to guard the east. If I can see them, I can take them out and make my way in. Once the shooting starts, you'll be able to bring a vehicle down the alley and pull up to the west side, flush to the building, and use it as your boost to make the roof. Clear as we go."

"I like it, but there's nothing to keep them from killing the girls," Tex said.

"I'm hoping that self-preservation trumps orders. Their first instinct should be to save themselves before they go running off to follow any directives. I'm game if you have a better plan, but I can't see any way to get in without being detected. By the time they know they're under attack, it's already over—I think it's our best play."

Tex was quiet for a long time before he said, "You're right. That's our play and our best option to avoid triggering mass murder. So, we're going to need to hit it hard and fast."

"Do you want to tell Eve, or should I?" Julian asked.

"I've got it. Prep your shit. I want to move as soon as you're ready," Tex said.

"Yes, sir."

Tex walked out, leaving Julian to get ready.

The body armor was already set up with the pouches where he liked them. Julian suspected Tex had something to do with that. Digging through the duffel, he finished setting up the vest with his radio, knife, and flashlight. He wasn't leaving anything to chance. Flipping open the weapons case, he found a new SIG P320 and M4 with an ACOG scope. *Oh, yeah.*

He was doing his function check when his toe struck something hard under the table. Taking a step back, Julian saw another duffel and weapons case. Elle's gear. Seeing it sitting there brought home the fact that she still wasn't here.

"If she were here, she'd be pissed we weren't already out the door." Tex's voice startled him.

"She's gone."

"We don't know that for sure. You can't make assumptions where Elle is concerned."

"What if she needs us?"

"Even so, she'd never get over us trading those girls' lives for hers. She'd demand that we finish the mission no matter the cost."

"I know. Still feels wrong."

"Welcome to my world. Elle's been asking me to make her a secondary priority for years. It never gets any easier.

But it does help that, in this case, she's right."

Julian watched the emotions play across Tex's face. He was struggling, too. "Alright. Ready to move. Let's finish this."

***

Twenty-three minutes later, they were in Oxon Hills, Maryland. The location was well planned by the traffickers. It was near major highways and a marina. Since it crossed state lines, it ensured jurisdictional battles if law enforcement got suspicious of their activities. Eve dropped Julian off a quarter of a mile away from the target and then took a preplanned route to her start point, giving him time to get into position.

"I'm set, Tex. Eve's pulling up now." Julian kept his voice low as he spoke into the radio. He was lying prone on the fire escape of an office building half a block away from the target.

"Set. Any movement yet?" Tex asked.

"I see a rover. Make that two. They just went on alert, scanning the front area. Our distraction seems to be working."

"Give it another minute to see if the guards increase in number. But, if you see a window, take it. I'll move on the first shot," Tex ordered.

"Roger that." Julian surveyed the entire eastern side of the storage lot, the lighting in the area and magnification of the ACOG sharpening everything. A third man came into view on the roof. He was crawling toward the front of the facility. "Got a man on the roof, southeast corner.

They'll have someone mirroring him on the northwest side…yep, got movement there, too, but no shot."

"Copy. Got a crash with their name on it."

"That will make a lovely housewarming gift. Very thoughtful of you," Julian said.

"What can I say. I'm all heart."

"Well, Mr. Sensitive, get ready to make your grand entrance." Julian did several quick rehearsals, sighting in on each target in turn. The railing helped obscure him from view but also complicated his shots. Returning his focus to the man on the roof, Julian breathed deep, steady, and even. On the natural pause, after letting out his third breath, he squeezed the trigger. Then, continuing with the pattern he practiced, he fired on targets two and then three.

A loud bang with a flash of light to the north was accompanied by a second one inside the facility. *Well, that should draw some attention.* Jumping up, Julian slid down the ladder of the fire escape and ran toward the facility. He watched the old Civic Eve was driving start up and bolt away from the curb. But, instead of leaving, as planned, she spun the wheel and drove straight at the gate.

What the hell? Julian put on a burst of speed just as the Civic crashed through the gate. The sound of metal grinding on metal made his teeth hurt. Climbing over the car, he shot an approaching guard and slid off the roof to the driver's side. Eve looked shaken but otherwise alright. She met his eyes and yelled, "I'm fine. Cleared you a path, now, go! Get Anne. I'll call Calloway."

"You need to move, Eve, now! I can't cover you and get to the girls. Does the car still work?" They'd underestimated how invested Eve was. Now, admirable as the effort was, she was a liability. Julian watched her struggle to get the vehicle in gear, but she managed. Eve put the car in reverse and stomped on the gas. The Civic lurched, the tires squealed, and she was off. To her credit, she didn't risk stopping to turn around, just kept going in reverse to get clear of the line of fire.

With her safe, Julian moved to the front office. That had to be where the team lead was monitoring the cameras and controlling the guard force. He approached the door. But, as he leaned in to grab the handle, it exploded. Wood shrapnel flew everywhere, including at his face. His skin burned, and his eyes watered, but he could still see. Not that he needed to see to hear the shotgun racking on the other side of the doorframe. He unclipped the flash grenade from his kit, pulled the pin, held it for a second, and then tossed it into the room.

He heard a curse and some movement before the grenade exploded. Rushing through the door, Julian hugged the wall on his right as he quartered the room to his left. There were two men inside, both disoriented by the flashbang. The one with the shotgun went down first, followed by his buddy.

The wall of monitors behind the bodies on the floor showed several rooms with women huddled on mattresses laid on the floor. The monitors were labeled with the unit numbers. Each unit had a guard on the inside. Scanning the other monitors, he found Tex making his way toward the correct row. "You've got company coming up on your left. Two men, side-by-side, shotguns. Be ready."

Julian heard two clicks in response, letting him know that Tex understood.

Below the monitors, Julian spotted a small, hand-held radio. Picking it up, he keyed the mic and watched the reaction inside of the units. The men on the screen all seemed to be listening to the open line—waiting. Time to take a page out of Elle's book. "Gentlemen, as you may be aware, tonight hasn't gone quite as planned." Julian paused when gunfire erupted. Watching the monitors, he saw Tex brutally neutralize the remaining rovers.

Returning to the radio, he continued, "Let me be more specific, for the three of you still alive, this is your chance to walk away. If the girls die, nothing is stopping us from leveling this place. So, do you want to live? Or join your friends?"

Julian watched the monitors for responses. Two of the men seemed to be wavering, but one was doubling down. He grabbed a hostage. It was Anne Daniels.

Elle had called the girl seasoned when they saw her at the trafficker's house. She'd had the chance to ask for help but didn't take it. Instead, she followed her captor's instructions, making him wonder about the depths to which she was damaged. Did Anne even exist anymore?

Only one way to find out.

"Tex, unit number 667. The guard has Anne as a hostage. I think he's going to use her as a human shield. The guards in 668 and 669 are still inside, but it doesn't look like they like the idea of putting their necks on the line."

"Let's do call-outs. Start with 667. That should take the fight out of the other two, and we can de-escalate things before HRT and emergency services get here," Tex said.

"Ready when you are."

"Go."

"Unit 667. We can see you. And we're ready. Go ahead and make your move. See what happens. Come on out."

The man on the screen stared at the camera, but then he started screaming at the girls and pressing his gun into Anne's head. The guy was unhinged.

"Your window of opportunity is closing 667. It's now or never."

The man snapped. He threw Anne to the ground and started shooting at the camera. He was a terrible shot. Round after round missed the target, giving Julian a front-row seat to the show. He didn't see where it came from—she may have taken it from the guard earlier—but suddenly, there was a knife in Anne's hand. Lunging to her feet, her face a mask of desperate rage, she buried the blade in his back.

"Tex, the guard is down. Anne stabbed him. Moving on." Julian said, "Unit 668. It's your turn. Your buddy in 667 wasn't very bright. Only two of you left now. Are you going to be the smart one?"

Nope.

The guard in 668 kicked open his door and ran out screaming and firing wildly. It was almost comedic watching Tex put a bullet in his head. He dropped without delay.

Getting back on the radio, Julian said, "It's over, unit 669. You're the last man standing. You can't complete your orders. And, if you try, you're a dead man." Sirens were approaching.

The man in unit 669 put his arms up in surrender. Then he pulled the radio from his belt, and a shaky voice crackled over the air, "I'm coming out. Don't shoot."

"Keep your hands where we can see them. No sudden movements," Julian ordered. "One coming out, Tex. En route to you now."

As soon as the door of unit 669 was open, Julian was on the move. Anne may not have been completely gone, but he didn't know about the other women. He wasn't going to let Tex navigate that potential minefield alone. He'd watch his six until backup arrived. Which, from the sounds of things, would be any minute.

CHAPTER 20

0900: Virginia Beach, Virginia

Three Weeks Later

Though it didn't quite feel like home, the beach house was transformed with his furniture all moved in. Having spent most of his adult life moving from rental to rental, he was used to the feeling and knew it would pass. Taking his coffee out to the deck, Julian sat on a lounge chair and tried to shake himself out of the funk he'd been in since they'd rescued Anne Daniels and the others.

They'd won. But they'd lost, too.

Julian had lost teammates before and struggled with moving on after deployments, but this was different. This was more than survivor's guilt. There were too many unanswered questions, and he couldn't let them go. The firestorm they'd started in D.C. with Congressman Daniels—Elle's idea for a distraction—was still going strong.

The scandal and the massive fire at the Earth Airport were just dying down. Some enterprising reporter pieced together Elle's connection, and things really went crazy from there. Calloway had Julian sequestered at CIA HQ with the rest of the team for the first few days to ride out the initial onslaught, and he personally oversaw their debriefs. Julian walked the Director through every moment leading up to the explosion at the hangar, hoping Calloway would find something he missed, some clue as to what happened to Elle. Nothing.

The fire at the airfield was out of control by the time the first responders arrived. It was burning hot enough to melt metal. Fire crews from all over the area came to help keep the blaze contained. Unfortunately, flaming debris had been hurled into the wooded area to the north, and it started to spread. By the time they got things under control, a couple of days had passed, and everything had turned to ash. The likelihood of finding any answers or bodies in the aftermath was almost non-existent.

After the Agency medics patched him up, and he'd finished answering all their questions. Director Calloway had sent him on his way. He'd been allowed to say goodbye to Tex, Eve, and Jack, but then the Director had reminded him about the particulars of his non-disclosure agreement. The team didn't exist, and he had nothing to do with any of this. He was supposed to go back to his life and rejoin his SEAL Team as though he'd just returned from deployment.

SEAL Team 2 had gotten back to the beach almost two weeks back, and, after gear turn in, they broke for some well-deserved post-deployment leave time. Julian had rotated back in during gear turn-in as though the past seven months had been uneventful. His platoon hadn't asked too many questions after he gave them his cover story—that he'd been assigned to a protective security detail for the State Department. Instead, they were more interested in busting his balls over his injuries, which he said were from a car crash.

The familiar post-deployment routine helped get him through the transition. He kept up the pretenses by following through with the beach house as planned. Getting ready for the move and the monotony of all the administrative crap gave him something to focus on. But now that everything was settled, his mind churned.

Julian sipped his coffee and watched the ocean, running through everything he could remember from his time with Elle. This was his new daily routine. He was missing something, he could feel it. The difference in her approach, saying goodbye, intentionally separating herself from everyone else. She'd had a plan that she'd kept to herself—he was sure. The question was, what? And did she succeed?

Deep in thought, Julian didn't realize he had company until he heard a car door shut. Glancing down at the driveway, he saw Tex leaning against the side of a classic Camaro.

Well, I'll be damned. Julian stood up and whistled appreciatively. "And here I thought you were a Prius man."

Tex laughed. "Are you going to let me in, Juliet, or am I only allowed to talk to you on your balcony?"

"Door's open. Got coffee in the kitchen." Julian walked back inside. He was filling a second mug when Tex entered.

"I don't have any cream or sugar, so you'll have to man up and drink it black."

"You have no appreciation for the finer things in life." Sitting down at a bar stool, Tex looked around and nodded in approval. "Not bad. I like it. Although, I hope you have the military clause in your rental agreement that will let you break the lease when you get new orders."

A little suspicious of that statement, Julian said, "That's standard for anyone on active duty, but I'm not supposed to PCS for another year. Why?"

Tex held up a large manila envelope. "Brought you a housewarming present." He tossed the envelope on the counter and picked up his coffee mug.

Julian opened it and pulled out a packet of papers. Orders? Reading the top page, he saw that he was being directed to detach from SEAL Team 2 and report for duty as part of a CNO Special Project. "What's this?"

"Well, you did such a great job on your last PSD that we wanted to make it a little more permanent. So, Calloway called in some favors with the Chief of Naval Operations and got you assigned to a special interagency task force. I hear the position comes with an automatic advancement to Senior Chief. You can spend your twilight tour there and roll right back into the position as a civilian if you choose, after you retire from the Navy."

"Um, wow, sounds interesting, and I'm honored. But what's the job? Who do I report to?"

"I have it on good authority that your new boss is one hell of a great guy. Handsome, charming, impeccable taste, a complete badass. Has a great car, too. He got to handpick his team, so he selected: a brilliant analyst named Eve James, a tech genius named Jack Paulson, and a world-class shooter—if he accepts the position."

Julian laughed to himself and took a minute to process the offer. He'd never considered leaving the Teams, didn't think an offer could ever tempt him enough. But now, he wasn't sure. "What would we be doing?"

"Our first mission is behind your orders. We have some unfinished business to attend to," Tex said.

Julian flipped the pages and found a dossier on Mahmud Hussein, target Number 3 on Elle's list to dismantle Daesh and the man responsible for her capture and torture. His resolve solidified. "I'm in. When do we get started?"

"As soon as we can get you checked out of your command and moved under mine. Now that you've accepted the position, those orders will be released through official Navy channels. The report NLT date is effective immediately. So, once the orders pop, you can begin your check-out process. It may raise a few eyebrows with your chain, but the orders are legit."

"It's Friday. I may catch someone in admin, but chances are it's a ghost town since most of the command is on leave until Monday. All my gear is turned in, and I can jam out a transfer FITREP and pick up my medical record from our corpsman without any issues. Other than the inevitable questions, I could knock it out in a day. Want me to meet you at HQ on Tuesday?"

Tex nodded. "Works for me. But we have something

else to do between now and then. Did you have any plans this weekend?"

"You're looking at it. Why?"

"We may have something—a lead on what happened to Elle. I could use another set of eyes."

Julian's heart rate accelerated, and he had to force himself not to get his hopes up. "What do you have?"

"Jet skis. Or, more to the point, a missing jet ski. There were two of them when Elle and I did our recon. So far, only one has been located. It's not much to go on. But, with Elle, any little detail could be something. I just want to be sure. This is off the books. Just you and me. I didn't even tell Eve and Jack. I didn't want to get their hopes up."

"I'm in. Think the boss will let us take his car?" Julian smiled.

"If you wipe your shoes off before you get in."

As they drove, Tex brought Julian up to speed on everything he'd missed since Calloway dismissed him. The Agency did a complete scrub of all its personnel in light of the Kim Daniels breach. Multiple people were still under investigation but, for those who had been cleared, they were in a rebuilding phase. That gave Tex the chance to recreate what Elle had done. It wasn't a hard sell since Calloway had been pushing him to be team lead, anyway.

Anne Daniels had gone through a horrific ordeal but somehow came out of it with some of her spirit intact. Her testimony sealed the fate of Seth Daniels and helped the police piece together how the traffickers did business. Seth had been there when Anne was taken. He'd met her at the train and then put her in the car with the traffickers and walked away. "Kim Daniels isn't going to fare much better.

In the early days of her captivity, Anne managed to get her hands on a cell phone and call her mother to beg for help. But Kim never reported it. She was in over her head and didn't see a way out. Her lawyer is going to plead out her case and avoid a trial."

"What about the ring leaders? Was Jack able to zero in on the seller? How about the buyers?" Julian asked.

"The seller, yes. And a couple of the buyers. But the rest disappeared. We turned over everything we had to the FBI, hoping they'll be able to do more with it."

"Why the FBI?"

"The IP addresses Jack tracked were all here in the U.S. They may have been spoofed, but it's all we had to go on. Puts it in the FBI's lane."

"How are Eve and Jack holding up?"

Tex sighed. "Jack hid it better, but they've both been hurting. The not knowing part is making it worse. I've caught them both combing through anything they could access from that day: data, images, news stories, official records. I should have stopped them, but I hoped they would find something. And I think they did.

"Eve found a story about a break-in at a vet clinic south of Gloucester, Virginia. The cops wrote it off as a junkie looking for drugs since the place was almost cleaned out of ketamine, but Jack pulled the stolen property claim and found that bandages, sutures, and antibiotics were taken along with the narcotics. The location didn't jive, though. Until I remembered the jet skis."

"You think Elle used a jet ski to get across the Chesapeake Bay without being seen. The break-in was a supply run. She wanted to deal with her wounds without being detected."

"It's just a theory, but it would work. And Elle is brazen and stubborn enough to do it."

"So, why hasn't Elle let us know she's alive?" Julian could see Tex tighten his grip around the wheel.

"I think it was her plan all along to disappear once the job was done. Elle believed that she was a lightning rod for trouble and that all her enemies would come crawling out of the woodwork now that she was exposed as a spy. I think the idea of another Tom Matthews was too much to handle."

Julian knew Tex was right. "It's been bothering me for weeks, and I keep playing everything she said over and over. She knew she wasn't coming back. Did Jack or Eve find anything else?"

"Maybe. When we first got back to HQ, Dr. Wise used the electric dead drop account he set up for Elle to let her know we were 'mission complete' and that she could come in. He's been checking it several times a day ever since.... Yesterday, he gave Jack access to the account. Jack worked his magic and pulled up the site activity log. There was a timestamp last week that Wise didn't think was his," Tex said.

"Wise thinks Elle accessed the account but didn't respond? Don't get me wrong. I want this to be real, but that's not much. Unless he kept a log of his own, it's possible Wise is just mistaken," Julian replied.

"Exactly. Which is why we're here doing some legwork. This place has been picked over by at least a dozen different organizations, so it's a long shot that we find anything, but I can't stop thinking about it now."

Tex drove them to the site. Yellow caution tape was everywhere, but it was otherwise deserted. He parked, and they got out and started walking through what was left of Earth Airport on foot.

Julian recounted the last time he saw Elle as they stood where the hangar used to be.

Tex listened as he surveyed the location.

"So, the only directions she could have gone would have been north or west. With a sniper on the roof, both options suck. But scaling the fence to the north of the hangar would have been suicide. Even if you had Olympic-level climbing abilities, you'd be presenting a perfect target for even a novice marksman. West it is then."

They walked through the skeleton of the second hangar and around the remnants of some smaller prefabricated buildings. On the far side of it all was a small brick structure. It was still in relatively good shape. Julian turned to gauge the distance back to the first hangar. "If Elle made it here before the explosion, she may have been shielded from at least some of the blast. I wasn't too much farther away than this. Maybe another fifty meters or so."

Nodding, Tex said, "Let's assume she did. And that she survived the blast wave. She would have been thrown and knocked unconscious, like you." He kept moving west, scanning the ground.

Julian followed, studying the terrain. The damage was less severe but still prevalent. One divot caught his eye. "Over there. What's that look like to you?"

Tex moved over to where Julian pointed and crouched down. "It's been too long to be sure, but something big hit the ground hard here. It doesn't fit the rest of the debris pattern. It could have been a body. Maybe Elle. Okay. Let's assume she survived the impact. She would have needed an escape route that took her away from the fire and any first responders."

"Elle's route in here was from the south. Her plan was to plant the decoys along the perimeter starting from the back and move toward the center of the airfield before jumping the fence. If things had gone as she planned, she should have been moving north by the time I saw her. But she was running out of the southwest, and the mercs were already on her. Something made Elle change her approach. If she'd been compromised by the jet skis, then she would've had no choice but to retreat, or attack. Retreat wasn't her style."

"Agreed. We'll keep retracing what we know about her movements. The southwest corner is our next stop," Tex said.

They walked in silence, both scrutinizing everything they saw for anything that may give them more information. It was late afternoon by the time they made it to the waterside of the airfield. The site was far enough away that it was unscathed by the destruction behind it. The water looked inviting beyond the fence. It would have been an idyllic scene if not for the razor wire topper on the fence or the large dome camera hanging from a pole.

Approaching the fence, a dark object caught Julian's eye. "Tex, over here." On the other side of the chain-link monstrosity was the floor mat from the SUV they had driven that night. Pointing to it, he said, "It's outside the fence."

Tex understood what he was getting at. If Elle had used it to get over the razor wire, then the mat would have shifted with her direction of travel, making it prone to fall on the side of the dismount. Bending down, Tex looked closer. "Some of those stains could be blood. We need to get over there."

Barbed wire sucked. Razor wire was worse. Julian hated having to deal with the stuff. It always seemed to catch him no matter how careful he was. But this time, he didn't care. They both took advantage of the pole with the camera on it to scale the top of the fence without having to navigate where to put their hands. It was a little awkward coming down, though. Swinging his body over the top, he let himself drop to the ground and had to roll on impact.

"Let's not do that again," Tex said.

"I'm good with that." Walking toward the water, Julian thought he could see lines dug into the grass that disappeared in the sand. Pointing, he asked, "What do you think?"

Tex studied them. "I think there was a jet ski here. Someone hit the beach with enough speed to propel them onto land. The bottom lodged here, forcing the rider to jump off and continue on foot."

Julian tried to contain his excitement, but this was the break they had been hoping for. "Between all the investigators and the ensuing media coverage, there's no way they just missed a jet ski parked here, under a camera. Someone took it that night."

"And I think we both know who," Tex agreed.

"She's alive, Tex." Relief coursed through him, and a weight lifted. He felt like he could cry.

Elle had put everyone through an emotional nightmare, and he should be furious, but he wasn't. He'd known what he was getting into. "We need to find her."

A slow smile lit up Tex's expression. "She's going to be so pissed."

"Yep. Can't wait."

EPILOGUE

1800: Memphis, Tennessee

Two Months Later

"I feel like these people need a lesson in respect," Cole said through a mouthful of mash potatoes. He reached for his drink and sucked up the remains of his Coke, which wasn't much. He slammed the beverage down and looked around the room like the angry heir apparent to a drug empire that he was.

John, his top enforcer, looked up from his turkey cranberry sandwich and shrugged. "Why bother. It's just a lousy diner."

"It's in my territory, so it's mine to do with as I please. These people know who I am. But I haven't been shown any respect since I walked in. They should be on their knees, anticipating my needs. Where's my fucking Coke? I don't see anyone bringing me one. Looks like my lessons haven't left enough of an impression. Punks who thought they were hard, the narcs and witnesses—they all thought they could cross me and live. They learned. Maybe I need to make a bigger example this time."

"What do you have in mind?" John asked.

"Kill them all. Then burn this shithole to the ground. Once word gets around, any place I walk into, I'll be treated like the king I am. And these fucking potatoes are lumpy." He shoved his plate, rising. "But first, a little fun. Make sure no one leaves."

"Yup," John said.

Cole stood up and walked over to the server who was working their section. As soon as the girl turned around, he backhanded her. She cried out as she fell to the ground from the force of the strike.

The rush he felt from her fear was incredible, and he wanted more. He pulled the gun out of his waistband and kicked the girl as he walked by. He relished how each person cowered as he passed, trying not to catch his eyes. *This is more like it.* "If I see a single cell phone, I'll shoot. Hands on the table."

He felt exhilarated, unstoppable, aroused. As he walked, he surveyed his options. He could have any of them, all of them. Who first? He stopped at a table with a family: a mother, father, and two teenage daughters. They looked like they wanted to be all grown up. Cole knew he was man enough to oblige them. He grabbed the girl closest and yanked her out of the booth.

"On your knees. Show Daddy how well you use that mouth." Her terror was turning him on. As she looked at her dad for help, Cole pointed his gun at the man. "Do as I say, or the old man gets a bullet to the face."

The girl was crying.

This was what he needed.

"Stop."

Cole turned to the woman who dared to speak. *There's always one.* She was in the corner booth with hands obediently on the table, and she wasn't even looking up at him. Short blonde hair stuck out under her ball cap, and a fresh scar ran along her cheekbone. Like she'd mouthed off before and was punished for it. But she obviously hadn't learned her place. "What did you say, bitch?"

The woman didn't responded or move.

Good, she should be scared. Cole threw the teenager away and walked over to put his gun against her head. That's when she moved. Fast.

What the fuck? Pain shot through Cole's wrist. Then, he felt pressure on the back of his neck propelling him forward into the—lightning bolts shot across his eyes as a sharp pain surged behind them. His forehead split on impact with the table. The pain worsened as blood blinded him, and then his ears started ringing from two loud explosions at close range.

Were those…gunshots? Where's my gun?

Cole felt his ribs crack from a kick that sent him sailing across the checkered floor. Then, a shadowy figure stood over him. He could hardly believe the whore from the corner booth had caused this, but it appeared to be the silhouette of a woman. It had to be her. Cole choked out the words, "You fucking bitch."

"Now, now. Language."

She cocked his gun.

"Do you know who I am? My men will fuck you up for this."

"You're Cole Mendez, the dime-a-dozen piece of shit Cartel lieutenant that thinks raping young girls and killing innocent people makes him special. And don't worry about the rest of your so-called men. If they're anything like your boyfriend was, this job is going to be easy."

"Who are you?"

"A problem solver. Freelance. And I'm done here." She aimed the gun at his face.

He could see the rifling inside the barrel. "No, wait, I can pay you!"

"I've already been paid. You're the first name on my list."

ACKNOWLEDGMENTS:

Real life has been the greatest source of inspiration for my stories. It's been over twenty years since I entered military service. The experiences I've had, and the people I've met have shaped my life in so many ways. And while a lot has changed in the past two decades, for me, it's always been about the people. I count myself as being exceptionally lucky to have been able to serve with individuals who, to this day, are like family to me. The dynamics between Elle, Tex, Eve, and Jack are reflective of some of my experiences, and those bonds hold a special place in my heart.

To my teams—from the early days with Special Projects Patrol Squadron One all the way through my career with Naval Special Warfare and in the Navy's expeditionary community—you know who you are…thank you. I would not hesitate to take a bullet for you, literally and figuratively. And my stories would not have the foundation they do without the time I've shared with each of you. Even after I retire, I will be there if you need me.

To fellow veteran authors who are now supporting me, even before I join them back in the civilian world:

A special thank you to Brian Andrews and Jeff Wilson for taking the time to welcome me to the thriller authors community and for supporting *Shadow War*. Thanks to "Father Bob," for always being there throughout my time in the Navy, and now as an author. To Stan R. Mitchell for being a friend and sounding board…and helping me figure out Twitter. And to Zach James for backing a fellow independent author.

To Mike Fullilove for helping make sure the details in the book were right, and all the team at DeliverFund for everything they do combating human trafficking.

I would also like to thank Best Thriller Books for all the support and for including me from the beginning. And a sincere note of gratitude to David Daitch and Katie Stone for giving me a look behind the scenes of their world and fueling my goals for post-military life.

As always, I would not have been able to do any of this without my husband Jake doing what he can to buy me time to write, and trying to help maintain what little sanity I have left. And, of course, thanks to my kids, Arya and Finn, for being my heart and soul while simultaneously giving me new gray hairs. Love you.

And I would be remiss not thanking Ken Atchity, Lisa Cerasoli, and the amazing team at Story Merchant Books. I appreciate all the support and guidance.

TO MY READERS

Thank you for reading Shadow War. Book reviews are often overlooked, but they are critical to helping authors gain visibility. Your feedback is important to me. Please take a moment to write an honest review on the e-retailer of your choice. Every review makes a difference. Have a great day.

—A. M. Adair

SHADOW WAR

Made in the USA
Middletown, DE
20 March 2022

62872584R00156